SOME LIKE IT HOTT

A STEAMY RUSH CREEK ROMANTIC COMEDY

SERENA BELL

1

NATALIE

It's a beautiful June day, I finally got a job, and between the sunshine and the victory, I feel like skipping up the street. Except I'm *really* not wearing the right bra.

Instead, I do an internal happy dance while walking like a calm, dignified adult toward Bon Chance Coffee to tell my boyfriend, Lloyd, my good news.

Lloyd works out of Bon Chance most days, with his coworker, Susie. We jokingly refer to it as his office and Susie as his work wife because he spends so much time with her.

Every once in a while, I feel a stab of jealousy, even if I'm the one making the joke, because Susie sees Lloyd more than I do, but he always reassures me that I get the best of him. *And the rest of me,* he says, generally right before he demonstrates how there's a part of him *only* I get. He showers me with reminders of how sexy he thinks I am and how much fun we have together, and at that point, I usually push the remaining self-doubt out of my head and let myself fall straight into the sexy fun-times.

I know we'll have sex tonight to celebrate my win. Because after a few painful months of being unemployed, today I took the first step on my Plan to Get Serious About a Career.

I tug open the front door of Bon Chance and enter the fray. It's still the coffee rush, with store owners from all around Bend's bustling downtown coming in for their fix—and a pastry or two.

I scan the coffee shop for Lloyd, but I don't see him.

There's a table of teenagers who seem thrilled to be done with school for the summer.

There's a happy couple holding hands. I can't see their faces, but they're curled in toward each other with that kind of new-love intimacy that gives me a hefty dose of warm fuzzies.

There's a table of gray-haired grandma types, laughing and chatting like they've known each other for decades.

There are two men in button-downs having a Very Earnest Business Meeting.

But no Lloyd.

I pull out my phone to text him. *Not at Bon Chance today??? I'm here and you're not!*

The man in the happy couple lifts his head from the new-love tilt and reaches for his phone, which is face down on the table.

Two things happen at once.

Alarm clouds his expression.

And I recognize his very, very familiar face.

Lloyd.

His eyes meet mine.

I'm frozen in place, all the joy and excitement I'd felt a few minutes ago washed out of me.

Lloyd lets go of Susie's hand. He says something to her, and her hand snaps to her side like a retracted tape measure. She turns around, and the look on her face—

It's raw, unfiltered guilt.

I take a step back.

Lloyd leaps up from the table and hurries toward me. "Natalie—"

"Don't," I say. "Don't."

I'm still backing up. I nearly run over two moms with their preschool-aged kids, who give me a dirty look and shepherd their precious ones out of my path. I trip over my own feet trying to push through the coffee shop door and stumble as I break free onto the Bend sidewalk.

"Natalie!" Lloyd says. "Natalie, stop. Please. Stop. Listen."

"I don't want to listen," I say. "I don't want to listen to you tell me that it didn't mean anything that you were holding hands with her. God, I've been so dumb. I can't believe I—"

I think about all the times I made Lloyd reassure me that there was nothing going on between him and Susie, when all along—

"There's nothing *like that* going on between me and Susie," he says. "I swear it. She's having a tough morning, and I was trying to give her some comfort. Susie and I— we're just—" He puts a hand on my arm. "I *swear* to you. There's nothing physical between us."

I freeze, not because of his hand on my arm but because

I've finally absorbed where he put the emphasis in that sentence. Not on *nothing*, but on *physical*. And something in my chest clenches, hard, and...breaks.

"Nothing *physical*," I repeat, barely managing to keep my voice from cracking.

"I swear it."

I will not cry. I will not. "I saw you, Lloyd. I walked in and I saw you together, and I didn't even recognize you because I was looking for my boyfriend who was here with his coworker, and what I saw was two people holding hands with their heads tilted close together, looking like they were head over heels for each other. So maybe you should explain that."

"It's not what you think. We're not—we haven't crossed any lines..." he says.

"Cheating doesn't have to be physical."

Lloyd's eyes flick guiltily from side to side. "It's not *cheating* to get different things from different people," he says. "You and I, we're *good* together."

I know he means *in bed*, and for the first time, it doesn't feel like a compliment. How many times has he told me I'm getting the best of him and the rest of him...and meant the leftovers?

I close my eyes and groan inwardly.

So, so many times.

"We have *fun* together, Natalie. Don't throw that away because there are some things I can talk about more easily with someone who isn't you. I mean, wouldn't you rather be the fun girl than the one who has to listen to me blather about heavy shit?"

He's earnest. He means it. He's looking at me with big

pleading eyes, while he tells me that I'm the sexy fun-times girl and she's the real thing.

God. Ow. All the joy I felt twenty minutes earlier has been sucked out of me, leaving behind the pain in my chest and a big, empty feeling.

"What you're saying," I say slowly, so there won't be any confusion, "is that you're in love with her but fucking me?"

He tilts his head, like he's giving it some thought. "I mean, that's a strong way to put it. I think you're emotional right now."

Oh, no, he didn't.

At least I'm not empty now. I'm *mad.*

He nods, like he's agreeing with himself. "If I were characterizing it, I'd say I'm getting different things from each of you. Which is what relationships are about, right? Different people give you different things. It's not healthy to get everything you need from one person."

Someday, I tell myself, *you will think of this moment and laugh.*

Today is not that day.

"Go to hell, Lloyd."

"Natalie," he says, both hands out. Placating.

"Don't," I say again.

The anger morphs back into pain—and fear—as I slowly register my situation.

My boyfriend is emotionally cheating on me.

My boyfriend is also my roommate—and the apartment where we live is my home.

My bank account is in the single digits. Not only do I not have the money to go back to school (step two in the

Get Serious About a Career Plan), but I have no money for first and last months' rent plus a security deposit.

There's *no* way I'm asking my parents for money or a place to stay. My pride won't let me. I know how they feel about me, my job, my choices. Maybe I wasn't supposed to know—

But I do.

Which means I have nowhere to live.

Unless...

Hmm.

I *do* have a job.

And—as far as I've been able to tell—a *very* nice new boss. Her name is Hanna, and she's a business-owning, name-taking badass. We hit it off from our first conversation.

Out of the wreckage of my plans comes a new idea, rising like a phoenix. Because, let's face it, I'm not one to sit around crying into my coffee. Also, I didn't have time to order coffee before my life went to shit.

I want to pick myself up, dust myself off, and move on, and I really, really don't want to give Lloyd the satisfaction of knowing about the ache in my chest. The one that says, sounding like my parents, *When are you going to get your life together, Natalie Archer?*

"Look," I say, pleased to discover my voice is nice and steady, despite the low-grade full-body tremor I'm fighting. "I came here to tell you I got the Hott Springs Eternal job. The resort-activities-coordinator job."

"That's amazing, Natalie! I know you were really excited about that one—"

I came here for Lloyd's praise, but now it's hollow, like all the times he told me how sexy and *fun* I was.

There's relief on his face; I can tell he thinks he's defused this *situation*. Defused me.

That would be a big, fat nope.

I spin through messages, looking for the contact I need. "I know it's in here somewhere," I mutter.

"What's in there?"

"My new boss's number. I need to call her."

"Why?"

I stare at him and say, "I want to ask her if I can get on-site housing."

"But you live with me," he says, giving me a doe-eyed look of hurt and confusion.

For a second I remember the day Lloyd asked me to move in with him. How good it felt to be asked, to be chosen. To be put first like that.

I wasn't first, though. I was, quite possibly, never first.

"No," I say, lifting the phone to my ear and listening to it ring through to Hanna's desk. Breathing through the hurt. Savoring the words even before I say them, as calmly as I can:

"I *lived* with you. Before I dumped your emotionally cheating ass."

2

PRESTON

"I'll be in touch in a day or so with next steps," I tell the CEO of MegaStar as I shake hands with him and his flunkies and escort them out of the Grantham-Hoyer conference room.

I exhale relief and inhale the big-money smell of imminent success as I head back to my office, where my assistant, Franklin, is waiting for me with his tablet in hand.

This office? Is my kingdom. Thick carpet, big mahogany desk, top-of-the-line office chair. Bookshelves full of finance books. Floor-to-ceiling windows overlooking the Manhattan and Brooklyn skylines, New York Harbor, and the East River. I am king of all I survey.

"Cut to the chase," I say. "Anything from Rhys?"

He shakes his head. "Nothing. I called him and left him the message about needing an answer ASAP."

"It's a sad day when your own brother won't return your calls."

Franklin raises his eyebrows. "Have you tried being nice to him?"

I glare at him.

"Just a question," he says, shrugging. "It's a strategy that might work for you...every once in a while."

"He's my brother. I don't have to be nice to him."

"Is there anyone you feel like you do need to be nice to?"

"I'm nice to you," I remind him.

He rolls his eyes. "You keep using that word. I do not think it means what you think it means," he says, Inigo-Montoya-of-*Princess-Bride* style.

Franklin, unlike my last assistant, can take the heat, which is one of the things I like best about him. He gives as good as he gets—which reminds me of my brothers, actually—and he's stellar at his job. Which is why if he says Rhys hasn't called, I know it's true.

If my last assistant had said it, I'd assume he lost the message.

"You did get..." Franklin consults his tablet. "Fourteen messages from Arthur Weggers."

"Shit." Arthur Weggers is my grandfather's lawyer and the absolute last person I want to hear from. "Can you give me the *too long; didn't read*?"

"Messages one through six: Can we please reschedule last week's meeting that you failed to attend?"

"Predictable." I had my reasons—very good reasons—for blowing off the meeting in Weggers's office. And I wouldn't expect him to walk away without a fight.

"There are also forty-three text messages and nine phone calls from people claiming to be your siblings also wanting to know what the hell you're thinking and what the fuck you think you're doing."

"I told them what I was thinking and what the fuck I'm doing," I say calmly. "I can't possibly leave New York right now with this deal and this promotion on the line. What about messages seven through fourteen from Weggers?"

"They say that if you don't call him to reschedule, he'll take some kind of unspecified action to compel you to show up."

I wave a hand. "We'll cross that bridge when we come to it. Not worried."

"Not that it's any of my business exactly, but what meeting did you fail to show up for?"

"It's none of your business."

"As predicted," he says, unruffled. "But don't you think I might be able to do more to help you make this dude Weggers disappear if I knew what I was dealing with?"

See, this is why I like Franklin. He doesn't take anything personally, and he always steps up.

Still, I hesitate before airing the laundry. Because...well, it's so...

Ridiculous.

But Franklin's right, and I will do anything to make Weggers disappear.

If only.

I gather myself for the reveal. "When my grandfather died last year, he left this will that said there would be a letter for each of my brothers—five of us in total. The letters would come at a time and date chosen by him, via Weggers. Two of them have been read already—Quinn's and Shane's. The letters contain elaborate instructions we have to comply with. We don't know when they'll be read or what the instructions are going to say, but if what happened to my two other brothers is any indication, mine's going to be extremely disruptive and require me to spend at least several weeks, if not months, in Oregon. Which is not what I need when I'm trying to seal this deal and score this promotion."

"Jesus," my assistant says. "That's—"

"Next-level manipulative bullshit from a dead guy I stopped talking to when I was twenty-one," I agree.

Franklin frowns. "I didn't even know dead guys could be manipulative."

"Me neither, until my grandfather died."

"But if you don't show up—"

I nod. Trust Franklin to immediately grasp the situation. "As far as I can tell, if I don't hear Weggers read the letter, the clock won't start ticking on whatever bullshit project I've been assigned postmortem. I'll have to pay the piper eventually, but hopefully it won't happen until I'm installed in that managing director's office, with you safely by my side."

It never hurts to remind people what's at stake for them. And indeed, Franklin's eyes get wider at the mention of the managing director's office that we will both be enjoying in a few short weeks.

"Why are we still talking about this?" I ask him.

"We're not," he says. "We're talking about how I'm about to confirm your Sagrada reservation and call your car for lunch with Damon and Ella."

"Good man." I grab my messenger bag—laptop inside—and head for the door.

As I step outside my office, I see a small gathering of people, and my mood—already sour—shifts for the worse.

One of the men is David Olafssen, who has been a thorn in my side since we were just-out-of-college analysts fighting for the best assignments. It's definitely no better now that we're seasoned senior veeps jockeying for the same promotion.

Because of the big client I just scored, I'm winning at the moment—assuming I can get this merger pushed through relatively quickly and before David comes up with something to outmaneuver me. And I know I can get it through—because I'm that good. I just need to keep my head down and work like a dog for a few more weeks, and I'll have done it.

I'll have proved, once and for all, that my grandfather was wrong. I can succeed in New York finance.

"Nice work, Hott," David calls out, and damn, it feels good. For about 2.2 seconds, until he says, "I'm hot, too, big man. Just brought in AmbiScreen."

Damn it. AmbiScreen is at least as big a player in tech as MegaStar is in entertainment, and a win right now could put David back in the running for the coveted promotion.

But I'm not worried.

I didn't get as far as I've gotten by letting a little competition put me off my game. In fact, I thrive on competition. I eat it for breakfast, lunch, and dinner.

I shrug. "Now things get fun," I say.

"Preston Hott," a voice says behind me, at about mid-back height. I spin and—

Oh, shit.

It's a short balding man wearing a cat-who-swallowed-the-canary expression.

Arthur Weggers, my late grandfather's irritating little

attorney, stands there with a sheet of cream paper in his hand. I recognize that cream paper. I have nightmares about that cream paper.

"How did you get in here?" I demand. Security should be better than that.

"You can thank me for that," David says cheerfully. "He was downstairs arguing with security, and I asked him what he was here for. When he said it was a legal matter concerning you, I knew you'd want me to send him up."

Of course David sent Weggers up. While there are plenty of people at Grantham-Hoyer who would be happy to sell me out, David has the most at stake—and he's happy to play dirty. The idea that a lawyer wanted to serve me with papers probably made his entire day.

I can't let Weggers read that letter.

"You want me to read it? Or do you want to?" Weggers asks, all wide-eyed innocence.

"I want to tear it into shreds and flush it down the toilet—"

"Let the man read your letter," David says, all mirth. He leans against the wall, the picture of relaxed nonchalance. Settling in for the show.

I grit my teeth.

"Thank you," Weggers says to David.

"Someone call security," I command, but I'm surrounded by people who are bored and jonesing for some drama—and who wouldn't mind if I got taken down a notch—so no one does.

In case Franklin hasn't heard the commotion, I pull out my phone and text him: *Get security up here right now.*

FRANKLIN

Already on their way.

Good man. But by the time security gets here, it might be too late. Because Weggers, who is normally all about the pomp and circumstance, opens his mouth and dives straight in. "'You're a stubborn bastard, just like your grand-dad. But all work and no play makes Preston a dull boy, wouldn't you agree?'"

There are snickers from David's lackeys. My workaholic reputation has never been a secret.

"I will sue your ass if you read one more word from that letter." But even as the words leave my mouth, I'm aware that in the last few minutes, I've gone from being a power broker to a heartsick kid fighting with a ghost. I hate this. I hate that my grandfather can reach out a bony finger from beyond the grave and erase all the years I spent proving myself.

"Go ahead," Weggers says. "I'll relish the fight." He drops his gaze to the letter again:

"'You have three months, starting with the reading of this letter—'"

I lunge for him, but he's surprisingly agile for an old guy and darts out of my way. Worse, David steps between me and Weggers. "Whoa. Whoa, man. I don't think you want to get physical about this, do you? Wouldn't look great when they're trying to decide whether to install you or me in that big, cushy new office, would it?"

And fuck, he's right. I glare but don't come at him again.

"'—to build an all-ages activity program at Hott Springs Eternal Resort.'" Weggers is breathless with excitement.

My chest deflates. My whole self deflates. Because let's face it. Even if he doesn't read another word, even if security drags him out of here right now and tosses him on the street, it's over. The letter is served, the charge is read, the clock starts now, and if I don't show up?

I'm the Hott brother who let our sister down.

That sucks.

Weggers, unaware that I've already ceded the victory, goes on. "'The program must provide an assortment of weekly activities that cater to wedding parties and attendees—some for adults, some for children, and some for families—and be vetted in a booth at the Rush Creek Summer Festival. See below for more details on the variety and number of programs.

"'You will live in Hott Springs Eternal housing starting no more than forty-eight hours from the reading of this letter until your task is complete.'"

David hoots. I didn't even know he had that sound in him. I've never seen him this amused. He's bent double, laughing.

"Or?" he says. "Or else? Or what?"

Weggers, delighted to have a new audience for his shenanigans, says, "Or the family business and the family land will belong to a mining company."

"You're not serious," David says, sobering. "That's tragic. What's the family business? Oil? Steel? Ranching?"

I've always wondered what people mean when they say something feels like a slow-motion train wreck, but now I know.

"It's a wedding and spa venue," Weggers pronounces.

"A wedding and spa venue!" David echoes. "Oh, well,

then. That's definitely important enough to take a month off from work!"

I hate him so much.

"It's my family's land," I say. "It's my sister's business."

David's eyebrows go way up. "Then you know what you have to do, don't you?" he asks, barely able to get the words out through his laughter.

"What's going on here?" a voice says behind me.

No.

It's Anjali. Our group head. The big boss. The one whose vote weighs biggest in the decision about whether David or I sit in the managing director's office starting next month.

Arthur Weggers looks from David to me to Anjali.

David grins.

"Anjali," he says, "I believe Preston needs a leave of absence, starting tomorrow."

3

PRESTON

"This is a terrible time for you to take a leave of absence."

Anjali—tall and slim in a gray pants suit, her long black hair wrapped up in a bun—delivers this piece of managerial doom and eyes me with concern.

"I know."

She raises her eyebrows. "You know I'm not the only decision-maker here. You need buy-in from the other managing directors. The board. I can back you—but I can't fight the tide if David is everyone else's clear winner." She frowns. "You can't take a month off while your deal and promotion are hanging in the balance."

We're in her office, which is *truly* the king's throne. Penthouse location, windows on three sides, views of Manhattan in all directions. Plusher carpet, bigger desk—though the same office chair because there is only so far you can go with office chairs. The next step would be a literal throne.

There is no bigger manifestation of power. She is the queen.

Someday, I will sit on that throne, too. But one step at a time. That's how I've made it this far. One step at a time, and no missteps.

Until my grandfather spoke from beyond the grave.

Now everything I've worked for is in jeopardy.

"I have to do this," I tell her. "This is my family's land. This is my sister's business."

She crosses her arms. "Explain to me how no one contested the will."

That's the question, isn't it?

"It was a divide-and-conquer thing," I say. "Only one of us got hit at a time. So first it was Quinn's problem, and he wanted to do it for my sister...and somehow none of us believed it was coming for us, too."

But there's more to it than that.

We all need to do this for Hanna. Because we *all* let her down. We all left her.

"Preston," Anjali says calmly, "if you score this deal and win this promotion, you can buy any land you want, anywhere. You can buy your sister any business she wants to run."

I picture how that would go over with Hanna.

Hanna, I've lost you Hott Springs Eternal and the family land, but no worries. I'm going to buy you some new land and throw a fuck ton of money at you, and you can start over. No big, right?

Like a lead balloon.

And it's not only that. I wish I could tell myself the land

means nothing, that I don't care if Blue Iron strips it for everything it's worth. But it will *never* mean nothing. It's part of me. In my blood.

I've rarely met anyone in New York City who understands what land means to those of us who grew up in the West. It's a different mindset. In Manhattan, 1.7 million people live in a land area of 22.83 square miles. That's about 73,000 residents per square mile, for those who math. Land, *schmand*.

Growing up, hundreds of acres were my personal stomping ground, and I can't imagine selling that land to someone who sees it as nothing more than an empty space to be stripped for heavy metals, gems, and minerals.

I don't point out to Anjali that I could already afford any land I wanted or buy my sister any business she wants to run, anywhere. In addition to climbing the finance ladder faster than any banker in Wall Street's remembered history —or so says the *Newer York Magazine*—I have invested well. Brilliantly, in fact.

I am swimming in money.

It's not about the money. It's never been about the money.

"I have to do this," I repeat. "And I *can* do this. I can take care of business in Rush Creek and still keep things rolling here. We're in a good spot with the merger. It's practically a done deal."

"You know better than to say that."

"I've *earned* the right to say that."

She shakes her head. "There's a reason every major world religion warns against pride, Preston." She sighs.

"Look. Olafssen is working on something big. Rumor has it he's aiming for an August-first announcement that's going to change the dynamics of the promotion situation radically in his favor."

"Shit," I say. "That's six weeks from now."

"Right. Exactly. You need to ink the MegaStar deal before that," she says. "Otherwise, you have zero chances of convincing the other managing directors and the board that you're their guy."

"No one can question my commitment to this job and this company," I say.

"I would never. You work harder than anyone I've ever met." She crosses her arms. "Too hard. We've talked about this, Preston. Your focus is always on the win, never on the people part of the equation. You get it done—but you don't make friends doing it."

I wave it off. Making friends has never been my goal. Installing myself on the throne has.

Anjali shakes her head. "It's going to come back to bite you in the ass, Preston. When people raise questions about your fitness for the promotions, it's always about culture match."

Culture match. In other words, *We like the other guy better.* "You know that's bullshit."

"'Course I do. We both know it's code for 'doesn't golf or go out for drinks or accept the Hamptons weekend invitation.' Code for 'doesn't look like us, think like us, or play the game *our way*—'" She scowls. "And I of all people know not everyone can play that game—and also that even when some of us do, it's still not enough." She crosses her arms.

"But, Pres, when was the last time you did anything besides work?"

"I went to my brother's fake bachelor party."

Her eyebrows go up. "Over a month ago. When was the last time you went out for drinks with coworkers? Or sat around in someone's office and ate takeout? Or tried to make yourself accessible to the junior analysts working for you?"

I wince. We both know the answer to that question: *Not in a long time.*

"Look," she says, "when the culture-match thing comes up, I say all the right things. I say we're not an old-boys' network anymore. What matters is who gets the work done. That there's no one in finance—hell, no one anywhere— who can get this job done like you can. That they should be glad you're serious about business, because you mint money."

"Thank you," I say.

"It's true," she says, picking up a stack of papers and moving them to the other side of her desk. "I'm just saying —and this is coming from someone who's been called an ice queen on multiple occasions—maybe you should lighten up a little. Let a few more people around you see your—" She cuts herself off.

"Were you about to say 'fun side'?"

She sighs. "Just—whatever it is you have to do in wherever the bumblefuck it is, get it done fast. Keep your eye on the ball, get your ass back in the office within the month, and if I say you need to show up in person, be on a plane before I can hang up."

"Got it," I say.

In my head, I can see my grandfather laughing, Satan with glowing eyes and evil mirth. One last obstacle thrown up in my path—but I won't let it stop me.

I'll fly across the country, save my sister's business, and be home to seal this deal.

4

NATALIE

By the time I start my new job a week after my coffee-shop encounter with Lloyd and Susie, I'm starting to feel more optimistic about things. My new boss, Hanna, hooked me up with a swanky room in the Hott Springs Eternal lodge; I've deleted all Lloyd's emails, texts, and photos; and I've pawned all the jewelry he gave me.

I'm not sleeping great, and I'm still a little weepy...but you can't have it all.

It's a short walk from the lodge to the main offices of HSE, which are located in what used to be the ranch house. It's a gorgeous old sprawling place, bare-log construction, huge wraparound front porch, giant windows—the works. I let myself in the front door, which tinkles merrily, and greet Julia, the dark-skinned woman with a Jamaican lilt to her words who staffs the reception desk.

"Oh, hey, Natalie. Congratulations on getting the job! I was rooting for you."

We'd had a nice long conversation when I interviewed,

about her four kids and seven grandkids and our shared love of *Yellowstone*. "Aw, thank you," I say.

"Hanna's ready for you," she tells me cheerfully, gesturing toward Hanna's office door.

I poke my head into Hanna's office and say, "Hey!"

"Oh, hi, Natalie. Come in."

I can tell right away that something's off. She doesn't sound as brimming with enthusiasm as she did when she called to let me know I had the job or when we talked about my lodging. But I tell myself it's nothing to do with me—probably a bridezilla situation from earlier in the morning—and step inside.

"Good to see you." She waves me into a chair across from her. "How'd move-in go?"

Most of the furniture in the apartment Lloyd and I shared belonged to him. I was able to drive all my possessions the half hour from Bend to Rush Creek in my battered Honda Fit.

"Easy-peasy. I love the room. I can't tell you how much I appreciate you helping me out with housing," I tell her. "There used to be lots of people I could crash with around here, but everyone I know has moved to Seattle or Portland or Boise. And my sister and her husband live in a tiny house. Literally—one-hundred-twenty square feet. They're all in on limiting environmental impact, but long-term guests—not so much."

Hanna shakes her head. "Yeah, no thanks. I don't love any of my siblings enough for that."

"My parents are still in Bend, but..." I wrinkle my nose.

She smiles at me. "But I take it they're not first on your list of roommates?"

"Exactly."

Hanna's petite and curvy, with round pink cheeks and very light skin. The combo of that and her dark hair gives her a kind of voluptuous-Snow-White-with-a-pixie-cut look that makes me want to chop off my own wild, curly hair. She's no-nonsense to the point of bluntness most of the time, which works for me. Plus, she's gone out of her way to help me, and we totally clicked in our interview.

"I'll have some paperwork for you to fill out, but first I wanted to have a word with you."

She rearranges a stack of papers, and I realize she's nervous. Which means the "something off" I observed when I first walked in? Probably *does* have to do with me.

Shit. "Everything okay?"

Should I not have asked for housing? Was it too much?

I don't know what I'll do if this job falls through. Things are over with Lloyd, and it's a huge understatement to say my parents aren't my first choice of roommates. Or maybe it's more accurate to say that the idea of asking them for any kind of favor makes me feel like throwing up. Which is why I have to save the money to go back to school.

And even if my housing situation weren't at stake, I want this job. Yeah, it's not on the long-term Get Serious path, but it's totally up my alley. I love people and I love, well, *fun*—and this is a job where I get to make sure people have fun. Nothing else I've applied for sounds like something I want to do.

"I have *so* many great ideas for how to make Hott Springs Eternal a true destination!" I blurt out, sounding like a bad cover letter—as if that's going to keep her from delivering whatever bad news is on the tip of her tongue.

She winces, and...I do, too. She looks away, and *shit. Shit shit shit.*

"It's complicated," she says, still not making eye contact. "Nothing to panic about, but there's a—twist."

"A twist," I repeat. That doesn't sound good.

"I don't know if you've heard anything about my grandfather—Fox Hott's—will... It's a legend in Rush Creek at this point."

I shake my head. "No, sorry."

She shakes her head, too. "It's fine, no worries. It's—okay, here's the thing. And God, Natalie, I'm really sorry about this bait and switch, but my hands are totally tied. I know I hired you to be the sole person in this position, but, well...God, how do I explain this?"

She's not making any sense, and apparently my face betrays my confusion and worry because she says, "Wait, let me start from the beginning."

But just then, her eyes leave my face and fix on something behind me. "Oh, hey," she says.

I turn to see a man standing in the office door, towing a rolling suitcase behind him. He's tall and broad-chested, wearing a gorgeous gray linen suit whose expensive tailoring flaunts the strength in his shoulders and biceps. His brown-and-burgundy power tie is cinched up tight against his strong, tanned throat. A half day of dark stubble coats his iron jaw, his cheekbones are carved from stone, and he's scowling like he just found out his bespoke-suit maker has gone out of business.

My mouth goes dry, and my thighs get hot.

I may have read a little too much "You liked *Fifty Shades*? Try this!" romance at a formative age.

My eyes go to his hands.

No ring.

Yes, I checked. The universe has spontaneously served me up a Hot Man in a Suit. I challenge any single, straight woman with a pulse not to try to figure out if this guy's married.

Although it's pointless.

Because things never work out between men like him and women like me. They're all business, and I'm a party. They take themselves and everything else seriously, and I'm still trying to figure out what I want to be when I grow up.

But it doesn't stop me from having to wipe imaginary drool from both corners of my mouth.

It might be the stern look and the crease between his dark eyebrows. The set of his jaw or the harsh twist of his lush mouth.

Whatever it is, I have to force my eyes away from him and back to my boss's face.

Which is pained.

Whatever the bad news is, it involves this man. And that makes sense because no matter what happens next, I already know he's bad news for me.

"Preston," Hanna says, "this is Natalie Archer. I've, er, hired her to be Hott Springs Eternal's activities coordinator."

His scowl deepens, making my heart beat faster, out of both fear and lust.

"That's unfortunate," he says.

Yikes.

Nice to meet you, too, Preston.

5

PRESTON

atalie's face falls. Which is understandable, considering my words. But I can't walk on eggshells here. I have less than a month to do the impossible, and she's the first obstacle.

"I assume Hanna told you the bad news."

"Preston, hang on," Hanna says.

"We're going to have to let you go."

"Jesus, Preston! Hang the fuck on!"

My sister is furious.

"You can't barge in here and start— Natalie, you're not being let go. Preston, sit the fuck down." Hanna buries her face in her hands momentarily. "There's a simple solution to this. Natalie, I'm sorry. My brother is—" She throws up her hands.

Natalie is taking all this surprisingly well. She stands up and holds her hand out to me. "Natalie Archer."

Her eyes—a cinnamon-brown color—are curious but not panicked. She's shorter than I am by almost a foot, with curly dark brown hair, and she's wearing a loose tunic-style top over a pair of leggings. A lot of her is hidden, but the part of my brain that never shuts up registers that her curves are...generous.

She's extremely attractive.

Which has no bearing whatsoever on the situation, so my brain and I agree to disregard it.

"This is my brother Preston Hott." Hanna's voice is aggrieved. "Like all my brothers, he's an acquired taste. Which can also be unacquired." She turns back to me and glares.

I glare back. Mergers and acquisitions is a good school for standing your ground.

"Don't listen to anything he says until he listens to what *I* have to say. First of all, he doesn't have the power to let you go because he doesn't actually *own this business*." She glares at me again. "I'm your boss, and he's..." She sighs. "He's basically the mother-in-law of the bride in this scenario."

Natalie bites her lip—holding back a smile, I think.

"So, you know how I was starting to tell you about the will?" Hanna asks Natalie, who nods. "Well, the will says—"

I break in because if I wait for Hanna to get there, we'll be here all day. "It says I have till the end of summer to create an activities program for Hott Springs Eternal, that I have to test the program offerings at the summer festival and receive at least a four-point-five rating on all of them, or—"

"Shut up and let me talk, Preston!" Hanna says. "This is my business, and the consequences are *mine* if you fuck it up, so let me talk!"

Natalie makes a sound that might be a choked laugh,

and I turn my glare on her. Surprisingly, she doesn't wither under it. She raises her eyebrows at me instead—a challenge.

And God help me, I've *never* been able to resist a challenge.

She has a pretty, round face and full, pink lips. My brain serves up an uninvited image of my thumb pressed against them to part them, and something in my groin tightens in a way that's completely inappropriate and absolutely distracting.

Fuck that.

I need to be totally focused here.

Hanna has been talking while my mind went on that rampage.

"—or we lose the family land and my business to a mining company. He has to produce the program, but the will absolutely doesn't say he has to do it without help or guidance, and you're the one who knows how to do this. So not only are you not let go, but you're going to help him—"

I cut my sister off. "No."

Natalie's eyes pop back to mine—wide, surprised, and definitely pissed.

I cross my arms. "I don't actually have till the end of summer. I have a month. And then I have to be back in New York. The program has to be done and tested by then. And in order to do that, I need this to be easy. Uncomplicated. The last thing I need is design by committee. Nothing personal," I tell Natalie. "You might be brilliant at your job. But I prefer to work alone."

It's *not* personal. She's just an obstacle to be removed from my path.

A very sexy obstacle, my brain says.

"No," Hanna says. Unfortunately, stubbornness is genetic, which means that all of us—every last Hott—inherited our grandfather's immovable-object personality *and* his irresistible force methods.

Hanna and I glare at each other. Hard.

"No," she says again. "*I* need this to be easy. Uncomplicated. And you are complicating it. Natalie knows what she's doing. You don't. And we need those four-point-fives."

"So I'm not fired?" Natalie asks.

There's a tease in her voice. Like she thinks this is *funny.* I turn and glare at her.

"No." Hanna sounds tired. "You're not fired. Now, let's talk about what's going to happen here. The two of you are going to work together and come up with an absolutely killer program, you're going to test it at the Rush Creek Summer Festival a month from now"—she looks at me as she says this—"because *someone* has to be back in New York, and we wouldn't want to stand in the way of"—she pulls finger quotes—"'one of the rising young titans of finance.' And we're going to start right now by brainstorming a list of ideas."

To her credit, Natalie takes this all in, nods, and pulls her phone out of a pocket in her tunic. Even though I want her out of here, I have to admire her spine. She's not backing down.

She swipes something open on her phone. "Okay, so my thought is we play up both the dude-ranch angle and the spa angle. Horseback rides. A mini rodeo on the weekends. Horseshoes, darts, skeet shooting, archery, lasso lessons—"

I put a hand up. "Do you have any idea of the liability issues surrounding that stuff?"

The corner of her mouth twitches. For the first time, she addresses me directly, her cinnamon eyes brimming with amusement. "That's what you got out of that? Liability issues?"

"I won't put my sister's business at risk."

Hanna makes a sound. Pretty sure it's a growl. "Let me be the judge of that," she commands. "Keep talking," she tells Natalie.

"Obviously we'll deal with the liability issues," Natalie says, addressing this to Hanna. "We could partner with some vendors, and then the legal issues would belong to them. Like pairing up with a riding school to make horseback rides available. Or the Wilder Adventures outfit could bring their rafting and paddleboarding options here. If an outside vendor offers the activity, the liability is theirs."

Hanna looks interested but not sold.

I shake my head. "We need to scale expectations way back for this one-month rollout. What you're talking about could work over months or a year, but it's not realistic for the short term."

"Makes sense," Natalie says calmly. "What's on your list?"

I swipe open my phone and look at the list I brainstormed on the plane. "Scavenger hunt, human knot, trivia, charades—what?" I demand because the twitch at the corner of Natalie's mouth has morphed into laughter, and I'm awash in irritation.

She darts a quick look at Hanna, who nods. Natalie squares her shoulders and says, "Those are eighties-era team-building activities, not upscale, stylish wedding-resort offerings. We have to think bigger."

"Those activities are classics because they *work*. And this is *exactly* what I didn't want to get into. Arguing about every little thing instead of getting it done. You see?" I say to Hanna. "This is why I think you should fire her. Because if we go down the path she's proposing, we'll never pull together a program by the end of the summer, let alone in a month." *And Hanna will lose the business and we'll lose the land. And then not only will I be exactly what grandfather said I was, I'll be what I've always most feared: the Hott who let this family down.*

But when I look at Hanna, far from nodding along, seeing the logic of my assertion, she's glaring at me with the force of a thousand fiery suns.

"Preston Barrett Hott. I did *not* sign up to get dragged into Granddad's bullshit and be a pawn in this ridiculous game while all of you get to act out your childhood crap all over Rush Creek." She crosses her arms and takes a deep breath, closing her eyes briefly before she speaks. "I didn't want to have to tell you or anyone this yet, but I'm *pregnant* again. So when I say I need this to be easy and uncomplicated—"

But she doesn't have to finish the sentence. It lands like a gut punch, and I'm sick to my stomach, remembering Hanna's last pregnancy and how she ended up with preeclampsia. I remember her clutching her head, her face washed of all color, and the hours pacing in the waiting room in the hospital while they brought her blood pressure under control.

She was fine. Eloise is fine. But I *never* want her or her unborn babies to go through that again.

"I'm sorry," I say quietly. "I'm an asshole."

Hanna scowls. "Agreed."

I'm half expecting Natalie to cosign, but she only says, "Hanna, I'm sorry I'm making this more difficult. Maybe I *should*, you know, recuse myself or whatever—"

"No," my sister says, more gently. "As he himself noted, Preston's been an asshole since he walked in here."

I should probably be glad she didn't say *since he was born.*

"You," she says to Natalie, "were just doing your job and trying to keep him from bombing out. And we *need* that from you, Preston's opinion to the contrary. So here's the deal. You"—she points at me—"are in charge because that's what the will says. But you"—she points at Natalie—"are the brains of this operation. Which means that you"—she points back at me—"need to basically follow her around like an obedient puppy, saying *Yes, ma'am.*"

"Puppies don't say—"

Her glare shuts me up. "And both of you had better keep whatever feelings you have about all of this to yourselves because I have had it up to here"—she gestures to her hairline—"and I don't have the time or mental energy to play games."

She turns to Natalie, and to my great pleasure, she gives her a stern-teacher look. "If you and my brother don't figure out a way to cooperate, I won't have a business—which means you won't have a job, and neither will I. And he can't do this on his own, obviously."

I start to protest, but Hanna aims a scowl at me that shuts me down.

"If you stay on and make this work," she continues to Natalie, "I'll give you a ten-thousand-dollar-raise and free housing for a year, in one of the new cabins. Regular employee rate after that but guaranteed for as long as you have the job."

Natalie bites her lip. White teeth, soft plump flesh. My body tightens again. Amazing that there's still a part of my brain with the energy to be turned on by someone who's essentially making my life miserable. Definitely a testament to the desert of my sex life.

Hanna stands. And scowls at both of us. "So come up with something that works, and come up with it fast. You can audition your first ten activities at the Wilder-Hott family party at my house a week from this coming Sunday. And you can start by both being here tomorrow morning at nine, in the conference room, to strategize."

Her scowl deepens. "And don't let me hear from *anyone* that you're making this difficult for each other."

6

———————

NATALIE

I walk slowly back to the lodge and my room while I contemplate my fate.

Apparently I am going to spend at least a month and possibly a whole summer working with a guy who in the space of half an hour went from being my ultimate sexual fantasy to my worst nightmare.

This should be fun.

By which I mean, this sucks.

I could quit.

I maybe *should* quit?

Except I have no place to go. No place to live. And no money with which to remedy the situation. No couch to crash on, unless I want to beg Lloyd or my parents.

My parents have never approved of the fact that I didn't go to college, my choice of careers, or pretty much anything else about me. In fact, the one thing they think I've ever done right is dating Lloyd.

I don't even want to tell them that he and I broke up.

And at the end of the rainbow (or shit show), there is a

pot of gold. A ten-thousand-dollar raise, no rent for a year, and guaranteed housing as long as I have the job.

Which means I'll be able to save for a degree or certificate; pick a lucrative, stable career; and finally stop being the fun-times girl, the slacker daughter, and the woman who can't quite get her shit together.

So. At least for a while, until I have enough money to be choosy, I'm going to be working with Mr. Asshole.

I take the elevator up to my room and hold my keycard to the touchpad on the door. It beeps and lights up green, and I turn the thick brushed-nickel doorknob and admire my new surroundings. I checked in yesterday, and I still haven't stopped gawking at the space.

Cream-colored walls. Exposed beams. Big, hewn-wood trim, including huge split-pane windows. A rustic armoire, a butter-soft brown leather arm chair, a Persian area rug, gorgeous kilim pillows. And the bed! Queen sized, with thick rough-cut head- and footboard, a luxurious cream-colored duvet, heaps of pillows, and a cozy-looking woven-wool blanket.

I didn't get a chance to unpack yesterday, so I take out my phone, cue up my favorite good-mood playlist, jam my wireless earbuds into my ears and start unpacking. I hang some clothes in the armoire. I toss my cosmetic bags onto the bathroom counter and stop to admire (again) the deep soaking tub and big-headed rain shower.

Free! I mean, long term, I'll be in a cabin, not the lodge, but still. For someone who thought she'd have to wait tables at three jobs to pay for school, this is...pretty damn amazing.

I toss T-shirts, underwear, and PJs into the dresser. I

stack a few thrillers neatly on the nightstand. Big Bob and Mack, my vibrators, go in the nightstand, too—Big Bob's cord curled up, Mack's glittery purple shaft nestled in his black velvet carrying bag. I treat my boys right.

I look at my watch. Just enough time to call for room service. I reach for the hotel room phone and order a steak salad and glass of wine. The woman on the other end of the line tells me fifteen to twenty minutes.

While I'm waiting, I could take a quick shower, get in my PJs, and start a new book. Get my mind off the events of the last week. Lloyd. Mr. Asshole. The fact that I have a week to come up with ten programs and test them out at a family party.

Just then, though, "Try Everything" by Shakira comes on. This song always makes me want to dance. It's my girl-power anthem, for when I'm feeling like I need a lift.

Time for a pump up.

I wiggle my hips. Do a little shimmy, setting the girls in motion. For better or for worse, and it depends on the day, my bra size delves deep into the alphabet, so there is *plenty* of motion. I grab the tall floor lamp and execute a pole maneuver. Okay, so floor lamps aren't intended for pole dancing, but I'll make it work.

Whew. I'm already sweating. I was in pretty good shape when I was working at the nursing home. I always took the stairs, never the elevator, and did a lot of active stuff with the residents. But since then, I've been spending too much time sitting at a desk combing through job listings and tweaking my resume to try to get results. I shed my socks, and then—okay, what the hell, I'm wearing a bra—tunic, too. Now I'm in just cropped black leggings and my favorite bra—black, plenty of support, but also loads of lace and frills.

I'm starting to feel more like myself.

I decide maybe I need my favorite party shoes. Hot-pink, spike-heeled, closed-toe sandals. They look great with tight, ankle-length jeans, but for now, they'll be fine with leggings.

YES.

I close the two tiny clasps and admire the strappy pink result.

Walk the Moon's "Work This Body" comes on, and *perfect.*

My hairbrush is a microphone, the lamp's my pole, this room is my court where I will beat whoever it is fair and square (*Lloyd*) and—

Damn. The ache is back.

Desperate times call for desperate measures. I turn the music up one more notch. I eye the desk.

It looks pretty sturdy.

I use the ottoman as a step, and—

Now I'm not in my room. Instead, I'm dancing on a bar in my spiky hot-pink heels. Mirror behind me.

I have my earbuds jammed in and my eyes closed, which is why it takes me a while to notice that—

Preston Hott is standing in the door of my room.

He's carved out of long, lean, well-proportioned muscle, which is more obvious now because he's taken off his suit jacket and draped it over the suitcase behind him, and his hand is frozen on one partially rolled sleeve. My eyes are drawn there tractor-beam style because that is quite possibly the best forearm I have *ever* seen. His tie is loose now, his hair rumpled—and holy shit, if he looked good buttoned up, he looks even better now.

Except I know he's the devil.

Plus he's caught me dancing on a hotel desk. And as previously noted, there's lots of me on display. Not to mention the spiky heels, the high drama lip syncing, the general bouncing, and all the *fuck you I'm powerful* gestures aimed at Lloyd.

Plus, mirror behind me, so: double view.

My cheeks go red hot.

Okay. Two options here.

Die of embarrassment, or…

Try my damnedest to play it cool.

I jam the pause button, tip an earbud out, and slide myself down from the bar—desk—with as much dignity as I can muster.

"I guess you're not room service," I say, managing a pretty convincing laugh. Because…well, it's a tiny bit funny, right?

Preston is definitely not laughing. He's scowling so hard it looks like he might break something. And as I watch, he reverses direction and rolls the sleeve back down, covering that delectable well-muscled, golden-tanned arm. As if to say, *This is not a situation where I can afford to relax.*

It makes me feel even more exposed. I scan the room for my top, but it's behind him, on the bed, and somehow it feels worse to let him know that I give a shit that he's seen me mostly naked.

"What are you doing in here?" I ask.

"They gave me this room key."

"Well, it's my room," I say.

"There must've been a computer glitch and they thought it was empty. I'll get another. Sorry to interrupt your—" He gestures in the general direction of my body, turning away as he does.

Thanks, dude.

"Dancing," I say. "I was *dancing*."

Then he looks back. "You're going to ruin that desk." His voice is deep and cultured and as chilly as the mist rising off ice.

My eyebrows go up. "Excuse me?"

"It's not made for wearing shoes on. Especially not shoes like—those. You're going to scratch the surface. Not to mention that I'm pretty sure they didn't test the desk for that kind of stress."

He didn't just say that.

He *did*. And I'm pretty sure I don't imagine that his eyes are moving over my whole body, a thorough perusal, or that he scowls again once he's taken me in.

Okay. Nope. That's...nope.

"Did you just make a crack about my weight?"

"No!" He has enough self-awareness to go red at that, and to look completely abashed. "God, no. I would never."

"Sounds an awful lot like you did."

"I was simply noting that the desktop wasn't made for jumping around on."

"*Dancing,*" I repeat. I can't decide if I want to laugh or cry.

"My point stands. You shouldn't be doing that. It's not safe. And the other hotel guests probably don't love the clomping."

Clomping? Fucker!

"And who are you, the hotel guest inspection team? They send you from room to room, making sure the guests aren't breaking any weird unwritten rules, like, *For God's sake, man, whatever you do, no dancing on the desk!*"

"I would think that would be self-evident without an actual written rule," he says darkly. He's backing up now, still scowling, but the suitcase wheel catches, and the case falls over. Something small and metallic tumbles out of his hand and hits the floor.

Reflexively, I bend and pick it up. Cuff link. The one missing from his dangling shirt sleeve. It's heavy. Expensive—onyx and probably platinum.

I drop the cuff link back into his palm.

His hand is big, the fingers long and elegant. He closes it around the plain onyx stud, then, with a practiced motion, shoots the cufflink home.

I imagine his internal monologue is something like, *Whew! Safe!*

"Your tie," I mock. "You need to tighten that up, too." I reach for the knot at his throat.

His eyes flash to mine, pre-storm dark, and I freeze as his pupils flare, darker, his gaze pinning me in place—

There's a knock at the door.

He jerks away and straightens to his full height.

"Put your shirt on." His voice is rough and commanding.

My mouth is so dry I can barely crack out words. "Um, what?"

He strides across the room, grabs my tunic and pushes it into my hands, scowling. His whole face is a thunder-cloud, his jaw set, a muscle ticking at the corner. "Just because I'm a good guy doesn't mean everyone who knocks at that door is."

Whether he's a good guy or not is debatable, but I take his point and pull the tunic over my head.

"There. You happy?"

If anything, his scowl deepens. "Not in the slightest."

Then he grabs the handle of his suitcase, tugs it toward the door, and launches himself out past the startled room service guy.

7

PRESTON

T he wheel of my suitcase catches on the carpet three more times before I make it to the elevator and bang the down button. So much for luxury brands.

The door glides open. I practically leap inside, exhaling heavily as the door slides shut.

What. The. Fuck. Was. That?

Natalie Archer, topless: pale, bare skin, gorgeous curves poured into a skimpy black lace bra and form-fitting leggings. Spike-heeled pink shoes I instantly wanted digging into my flanks.

Plus a no-fucks-to-give attitude that shouldn't have made the ensemble even sexier but somehow did.

And I was a certified dick about the situation. Not for the first time today.

Finding my room already occupied was the last straw on a miserable day. It was like the universe knew my life was a temporary shit show and was chiming in with helpful additions. Even before the showdown in Hanna's office, my jet sat on the runway for more than two hours while the best mechanics money can buy wrestled with the landing gear. The state-of-the-art airplane toilets got clogged, and the premium on-board fridge turned out to have died (no food). My driver didn't show up in Bend, and the high-priced car service flailed like amateurs until I gave up and rented the best thing I could find at the tiny airport.

You could call an Uber, Franklin informed me while I waited for the rental company to produce my car, cursing expensive things that don't do what you've paid a fortune for them to do.

I don't have the app.

Download it.

I'd have to set up an account and create a password.

Franklin's sigh suggested weary patience. *I think this might be an example of first-world, rich-people problems*

I think you might be right, I said tiredly.

And then, when I finally arrived, there was *her.*

Obstacle-ing the shit out of my already-complicated-enough life.

Dancing on the fucking desk.

Reaching for my tie and making all the blood in my entire body flee for the equator.

All I want is to keep this as simple as possible. Occupy my room. Dispatch the stupid will. Get the hell out of dodge. No complications. No distractions. And definitely, absolutely, *no temptations.*

And instead, here she is, making everything hard.

Not like *that.*

But yeah, definitely like that.

Obviously my grandfather's point about all work and no play had some validity: It's been *way* too long since I got laid.

And there's nothing I hate more than my grandfather being right, even a little bit.

The elevator touches down on the main floor and opens. I head to the desk, where a pretty woman with short blond hair greets me for the second time. She's not someone I've met on my previous visits to Rush Creek, so she must be new-ish.

I slide my keycard across the dark wood desktop. "This room is already occupied."

"Oh, I'm so sorry! I don't know how that happened, Mr. Hott!"

"It was awkward."

She winces. "I can imagine. I'm so, so sorry. We can—comp you breakfast. And a drink at the bar—"

"I'm not a paying guest," I remind her. "All those things are already free."

"Right," she says. "Well..."

She falls silent.

"Just fix it," I say.

"Of course, Mr. Hott. Right away."

She's back a moment later with a new key card.

"You're sure this one is unoccupied."

"Ninety-nine point..." She hesitates. "Two?"

"Good enough," I say. "Hopefully I won't see you again tonight."

"Hopefully!" she says, then clasps her hand over her

mouth. "Of course, Mr. Hott, we are *always* happy to see you and serve you in any way we—

I raise my eyebrows skeptically, and she trails off.

"Good night, Mr. Hott," she says, more subdued.

I don't look at my room number until I'm standing in front of the numbered elevator buttons, and then I realize: It's the room next to the one I was just in.

I go back to the desk. I don't think it's my imagination that she cringes slightly as I approach. Probably because I look like Dr. Doom, my expression reflecting my current attitude.

"I don't suppose you have any other rooms left?" I ask.

She presses her lips together and shakes her head.

"Or you could trade this for a room reserved for someone who hasn't checked in yet?"

"I'm sorry, sir." Now she actually *sounds* sorry. "But as you know, it's wedding season, and that room I just gave you is only open because a bridesmaid no-showed. It's literally the last room we have left."

Of course it is.

"There might be a cancellation at some point?" she says doubtfully. "They're rare in summer, but it's...possible?"

"Could you put me on the waiting list?"

"Of course, sir, but it's—it's a long waiting list."

I frown.

"We could bump you to the top of the list, of course, sir," she says quickly.

She hastily grabs for a pencil and scribbles something on a sticky note. I eye it suspiciously. A hundred bucks says the person on the next shift tosses that scrap of paper.

"Is that Hott Springs Eternal's system for keeping notes?" I ask.

"There's no way for the computer to remind us," she says, biting her lip apologetically. "If I edit the room entry in the reservation software, no one will see it till you check out. You can check back in from time to time, see if something's opened up."

I make a mental reminder to let Hanna know she needs to research alternative systems—and one to come back on Monday and follow up about the waiting list.

I ride the elevator back to the floor I came from and let myself into the room next to *hers*.

It's the twin to the one I just saw. Same cream-colored walls and exposed beams, same queen bed with chunky roughly hewn wood, same armoire, same woven blankets, rugs, and pillows.

I toss my suitcase onto the bed and unpack my things— it doesn't take long. And then I settle myself on the bed and turn on the TV.

But even with the TV on, I can hear her next door. I can't hear her music because of the earbuds, but the sound of her shoes on the desk reverberates through my brain.

I can see her in my mind's eye.

Round face; wild curly dark hair; curvy, generous body. What was left of her clothing hid nothing—not the plump triangle where her thighs met nor the glorious swerve of her ass, and *definitely* not the nipples poking hard against the flimsy black lace of her bra.

She *was* dancing like no one was watching, her hips rocking and swaying, every soft, pale lickable part of her in motion.

I can picture her moments later, too, standing in front of me, one hip cocked slightly to the side, a teasing smile on her face, hand reaching for my tie. Confident and challenging, the kind of woman who could be caught dancing topless by her boss's brother and laugh about it.

I close my eyes, but I can still see her, a snapshot memory, on the inside of my lids.

8

PRESTON

Get in, get out, get it done.

That's my mantra as I step into the Hott Springs Eternal conference room the next morning.

The activities calendar doesn't need to be perfect, just good enough to earn a 4.5 average.

I'm used to dotting every *i* and crossing every *t* on multi-billion-dollar deals. A 4.5 on a bunch of cruise ship activity sessions feels entirely doable.

Get in, get out, get it done.

I settle myself at the head of the table. I'm early.

I check my email, my texts. I check and recheck some numbers one of the junior analysts ran for me.

They still add up. The third time, too—*is* dotted, *ts* crossed.

Hanna sticks her head in. "Be nice to her," she says.

"I'm always nice."

My sister rolls her eyes. I seem to be getting that a lot lately.

She leans against the door frame. "Did Kali come back to Rush Creek with you this time?"

Damn. I'd been hoping since she hadn't asked about my ex-wife yet, we'd avoid this whole topic. No such luck.

"She's super busy," I say. Which is true, as far as it goes.

So, yeah: I may have neglected to mention to my family that I'm no longer married. And the longer I don't mention it, the bigger of a thing it becomes. How do you tell your family that you made it all the way to signed divorce papers without mentioning to them that your marriage was fucked?

Hanna crosses her arms. Stares at me with icy blue eyes that remind me of our grandfather's. Eyes that see right through my lies.

I almost crack, except that right then Natalie pokes her head in the door, smiling, curls bobbing. "Hey!"

"You're late," I tell her.

"Preston," Hanna growls.

"Go," I tell her, pointing at the door, and, glaring at me the whole while, she does.

Natalie consults her phone. "I'm not late. There's a five-minute grace period on everything, and I'm only two minutes past that, which isn't even five minutes late."

"Early is on time; on time is late; and late is unacceptable," I counter.

She shakes her head. "Early is early. On time is on time. And a little late is just being human."

I frown. "No one ever said that."

"They should have."

She's not remotely intimidated by me. Which is foreign and...also intriguing.

She steps all the way into the conference room. She's wearing a pair of capri pants and a blue scoop-necked top. I try—unsuccessfully—not to notice how the pants fit snugly over her perfect ass and the top swerves suggestively over her way-more-than-a-handful tits. I make an internal note: Tonight, I'm Tindering and blowing off some steam, something I haven't done in months. I've lost track, which tells me all I need to know. Enough of this bullshit.

Her hands are empty.

"Where's your laptop?" I demand.

Natalie shrugs. "I don't have one. I'll take notes on my phone."

"You can't view a whole spreadsheet on your phone."

"I wasn't planning on viewing any spreadsheets." She lowers her voice to a murmur. "Also, are we going to pretend you didn't see me dancing in my bra?"

"Yes," I say, because that is the only rational response to the situation. Nothing good could possibly come of dwelling on that moment. Of remembering what I saw. Efficiency is the name of this game.

"Wooo—okay, then," she says and plops down into the chair next to mine. It's around the corner, but she's close enough that I pick up her cinnamon-apple scent. I scoot my chair away.

"We *will* need spreadsheets," I say. "To keep lists of activities and to make schedules. I took to heart what you said about eighties team-building activities."

She looks startled.

"I can compromise," I say grumpily.

"Make sure you do," says a stern voice behind me, and I turn to see Hanna, head poked into the conference room again. Which, in fairness, I probably deserve after my behavior yesterday. But today I'm turning over a new leaf. It's the *whatever will make this happen fastest* leaf.

"Quit it," I tell my sister, and her head disappears. I turn back to Natalie. "I brought some new ideas."

She raises an eyebrow.

"Bingo. And paint with gems."

She squints at me. "Bingo," she repeats dubiously.

"Hanna told me where you worked before this. There was an old calendar of events online, so I studied it. I figured those things were already vetted by you, so we should be able to get to consensus quickly."

Her forehead wrinkles. "But that was a nursing home. This is a high-end dude-ranch-style wedding resort." She purses her lips. "I have an idea. What if we do what I said yesterday and mostly partner with programs that already exist but then throw in some additional things that are relatively easy to implement. Basically then we'd just have to go vet the ones we wanted to partner with and spend the rest of our time putting together the others."

"Examples?"

"For partnerships, I'm thinking the horseback riding, plus a few things Wilder Adventures could make happen for us—Hanna can vouch for Wilder, so we'd basically just need to talk to the guys in charge and see what they're interested in doing." She looks down at her phone for a moment. "Also, axe throwing—"

"Nothing with deadly weapons."

For a second her eyes meet mine, fire in them. I think she's going to argue, and I discover I'm looking forward to it. But then she drops her gaze. "Okay," she concedes. "No deadly weapons. What about a pop-up rage room? I think we could arrange with a vendor to bring that here."

I roll my eyes but don't protest because Hanna is still making occasional passes through the hall outside our room.

"If we had a splatter room…" she says wistfully. "Maybe we could improvise that? Or set up basically the equivalent of an outdoor one?"

I flinch. "What the hell is a splatter room?"

"It's a room where all the walls are lined and you can make a complete mess. If we wanted to do body painting, for example—"

"*Body painting?*"

"Yeah, like couples could put paint all over each other's—"

I wave my hand because I need that image in my head like I need—well. I don't need it. No one will be painting anyone else's body.

"Or Jell-O wrestling."

"*Jell-O wrestling?*"

"It's *really* fun."

"I'm going to take your word for that," I say, trying extremely hard not to picture *anyone* in a tub of Jell-O.

She bites her plump lip; she's definitely trying not to smile. "Okay, what about…improv workshops, a casino night—we might even be able to get Five Rivers to come in and do it. Rock climbing—I noticed there are some nice faces on the property, and I think the Wilders are certified—"

"You really do want us to get sued."

"That's what the partnerships are for," she says. "I won't

do anything that could hurt Hott Springs Eternal or your sister. I need this to work. I need this job."

She says it so earnestly, there must be a story in there. What makes this woman tick? She seems so unflappable, but she apparently wants this job enough to put up with me. Before I can ask *Why is it so important to you?* she says, "You need a four-point-five, so therefore, you need activities that are actually fun."

"Who thinks that stuff is fun? Improv? Body painting?"

Her eyes and mouth are both wide with disbelief. "Everyone?"

"We're going to have to agree to disagree," I tell her. "There's nothing fun about risking your life or your pride or getting covered with paint."

She buries her face in her hands. I can see Hanna coming back our way. Quickly, I say, "Okay. Okay. So what's the plan?"

Hanna's right outside the door.

"Meet me at Green Will Lake Campground Monday night at seven thirty," Natalie says. "We're going to pay a visit to Brody's Boats."

"What's Brody's Boats?"

"You'll see. Just meet me and follow my lead."

Hanna passes by, out of audio range.

Natalie whispers, "Like an obedient puppy."

My gaze flashes to hers. She raises her eyebrows and smirks at me, and God help me, I almost—almost—smile.

9

NATALIE

"Thank you so much for making time for us," I tell Rachel Wilder, who, with her husband, Brody, runs Brody's Boats. It's the boating-charter division of Wilder Adventures, the business run by Hanna's husband, Easton, and his four brothers.

"Of course!" Rachel says. "We prepared a sampler for you of what we offer."

Rachel's maybe ten years older than I am, with warm medium-brown skin and thick dark brown hair pulled back in a ponytail. She wears a pair of mom jeans and a hot-pink T-shirt with purple lettering that says, *Sorry if I'm not repressed enough for you.* Makes sense, since Hanna told me that Rachel is a certified sex counselor who runs a sex-education nonprofit and still finds time to maintain a small sex therapy practice.

Brody offers me a warm smile and holds his hand out for a shake. He's wearing motorcycle boots and a ripped T-shirt and jeans, and his arms are elaborately tattooed—rain droplets on glass, fish, waves.

Okay, I get it: water-themed.

"We're excited about the possibility of a partnership with Hott Springs Eternal," Brody says. "Did you bring Hanna along?"

"No, I, uh—"

"She brought me," Preston says, strolling up. He'd lingered in his car to drop into a "very important phone call with New York"—never mind that New York should have been asleep hours ago—and I teasingly reminded him that *on time is late*, before I remembered that he doesn't have a sense of humor.

Still, the scowl was its own reward.

Why is annoying Preston Hott so much fun for me?

Despite the fact that we're about to board a boat, Preston is *still* wearing office clothes. In this case, a gray-and-white seersucker suit that on anyone else would look ridiculous. On Preston it's sin walking.

I swallow saliva that otherwise threatens to become drool. "I don't know if you heard, but Preston and I are working together for a few weeks."

Magically, my voice is unaffected by lust.

"Is this *will* stuff, dude?" Brody asks as Preston does the manly swat-across-the-back/side-hug thing with him.

"Will bullshit," Preston confirms.

"Ah. Okay," Rachel says, eyes roving over the two of us with a new spark of curiosity. "This presentation was optimized for an audience of women, but—"

"But Rachel can improvise like a boss," Brody interjects. "So no worries." He casts an eye at Preston's outfit. "Come on aboard."

We board his boat—a decent-sized fishing boat that

Brody tells us is a "thirty-five foot Scout"—and sets us up in the large open bow on cushioned benches. It's really nice. Rachel sits down with us, a small crate at her side, while Brody heads into the cockpit.

He cruises us out a short way onto the lake, which is—beautiful. It's surrounded by mountains, a few of which still boast snow coverage on their highest peaks. The sun is low enough in the sky to barely kiss the tops of the trees at the lake's edge, and a breeze blows its woodsy scent out to us. I breathe deeply. I can definitely see HSE's guests loving this.

"Basically," Rachel says, "we can host just about anything on board the boat. We regularly do book clubs, product parties, wine tastings, bachelorette parties, craft nights, a whole variety of other girls' nights out. And we'd be happy to do any-slash-all of those things for Hott Springs Eternal." She spreads her hands. "But I also thought it would be great for us to do something branded specifically for HSE. That's what I've prepared for you. I'm tentatively calling it the Wedding Launch." She looks from Preston to me and back again, opens her mouth, closes it again, and shrugs. "Apologies in advance if this is"—she looks directly at Preston—"not what you were expecting when you showed up tonight."

She reaches into her crate and pulls out a bottle of champagne, which she adeptly pours into two flutes and offers to Preston and me. Next she hands us each a small plate on which she arranges a few extremely classy appetizers. And a small cocktail napkin.

She doesn't take any for herself.

Uh, I see. We're the newlyweds.

Preston doesn't look at me. I don't look at him. I sip my champagne.

"Obviously we'd aim to do it a bit later at night. Under the stars. And we'd go out further on the lake, where the mountains are more visible. It's basically a honeymoon kick-starter."

"'Honeymoon Kick-Starter' would be a cute name, too," I say, sipping my champagne and trying as hard as possible to act like I knew I'd be pretending to be Preston's new wife when we boarded this boat.

"Once the couple is settled in with food, I'd offer a just-for-two version of my classic one-hour presentation." She leans down again and pulls some items out of the crate. "I start with candles and oils and lotions, and then if people are open to it, we talk about reciprocity and intimacy and..."

Without breaking stride, Rachel takes our champagne glasses and plates and sets them in clever holders clearly optimized for on-board dining, then hands us some of the contents of the crate.

I look down to discover I'm holding a vivid red two-headed vibrator and a set of bright pink Kegel balls.

I check the contents of Preston's hands.

Yup.

Fleshlight in one, warming gel in the other.

He has a loose, almost panicked grip on his items, like he's holding two hot potatoes. Like they're burning his skin.

My eyes rise to his face. A blush darkens his already naturally dusky-tan cheeks. I can't tug my gaze away from it or the way it spreads down to his neck. I want to trace the line of red with my fingertip and ask him what's got him so hot and bothered.

But only to annoy him.

He's given me a hard time since the first moment we crossed paths, and I want to push back.

That's the *only* reason I hold up the clit-and-G-spot vibrator and say, "Oh, I have one like this back at the lodge!"

And then turn it on and press the vibrations against my fingertips.

10

___

PRESTON

My face is hot, which is remarkable only because I'm pretty sure all the blood in my entire body is in my cock.

Natalie owns something like that—with the shaft on one side and the small, forked tip on the other side—that she uses...

I have to make myself stop because I absolutely cannot finish that sentence and survive.

I carefully set down the Fleshlight and the warming gel and pick up my champagne and small plate, because as awkward as it felt to role-play being newlyweds with Natalie, it was way, way better than holding sex toys while she buzzes the tips of her fingers in a way that feels down-right...pornographic.

"What about you, Preston?" Natalie asks, innocently. "Do you have one of those at home?" She gestures—with the still buzzing vibrator—at the Fleshlight.

No one is playful with me. My marriage was never playful. I don't think that for most of it, Kali liked me enough to want to play.

Even my brothers know better than to mess with me. They might rib me here and there, but they treat me with the wariness you reserve for someone who finds it hard to laugh at himself.

Natalie's teasing feels good in more ways than one.

And yet when I open my mouth, I drop a single, blunt, "No."

A small furrow appears in Rachel's brow. She looks from Natalie to me and back again, lifting her shoulder in a small shrug. "Well," she says cheerfully, "it's a lot of fun. But I'm not here to sell you on the products—just the services. You know where to find me if you decide to invest." Then she shrugs again. "And since you're not actually a couple, I won't subject you to my intimacy lecture. Just know that it's good. Survey after survey says it increases the number of orgasms attendees have per week." She winks.

I choose that unfortunate moment to glance at Natalie. She's watching me right back. Our eyes meet—and we both look away quickly.

Rachel extends her hand, and Natalie returns the vibrator to her but holds on to the Kegel balls, like she's reluctant to let them go. "I'm going to take a set of these," she tells Rachel. "I've always been curious."

"Oh, they're lots of fun," Rachel says. "I'll set aside some for you." She grins. "We can talk another time about strategies."

Strategies. Strategies that will involve Natalie parting her legs and easing those balls into her—

"Preston, what about you?" Rachel asks.

"Oh. No, thank you. No product for me," I say hastily.

"No, I was asking"—she does an admirable job of keeping a straight face—"what you think about the concept of the Wedding Launch?"

If my face gets any hotter, it will burst into flame. And *fuck me*. I'm not a twelve-year-old boy in sex-ed class; I'm a grown man who—blurted lies aside—*definitely* has a Fleshlight at home, used a vibrator with his ex-wife, and thinks that sex toys are basically cool.

I just wasn't expecting to be blindsided by them...or my curiosity about what Natalie does with hers. But no way am I going to let her know that.

"I think it's great," I say, pulling it together. "Fun and educational and obviously an important topic."

I actually manage to sound semi-human.

"And obviously the launch would be purely optional for newlyweds! Not everyone's comfortable with all this," Rachel says, spreading a hand to indicate her product. "But it's my hope that I could start a lifelong conversation about mutual pleasure."

"Absolutely," I say. "I'm a big fan of mutual pleasure."

Beside me, Natalie makes a sound. I don't think it's a laugh, but it couldn't have been anything else, right?

Rachel settles back on her bench. "Don't let the food and champagne go to waste." She hands Natalie back her plate and glass, and with deep gratitude, I swallow half my glass of champagne in one gulp, glad to have something to do with my hands.

Rachel tilts her head. "Let's talk about what else you might be interested in, programming-wise. Book clubs are out because you don't have the lead time, but we could do wine tastings, nature cruises, or any of the other things I mentioned."

Natalie nods. "Can you get me a proposal with pricing for the Wedding Launch? I'm thinking we could have two per week, one right before and one right after the weekend? If you have the availability."

"I have a great team of educators, and we've got a good-sized fleet at this point," Rachel says. "I can't be at every party myself, but I can definitely make them happen."

"And maybe include in the proposal, but broken out so I can see them separately, one nature cruise and one wine tasting per week?"

"Absolutely," Rachel says.

"Oh, and—can you demo the possible sessions at the Wilder-Hott party this weekend?" Natalie asks. She explains that Hanna has asked for the demo, not telling Rachel the story of how I antagonized her into demanding it. I...appreciate that.

"Absolutely," Rachel says.

They sort out timing and details, and business concluded, Brody navigates us back to the dock. The sun has dipped below tree level now, and the breeze is cool. I try not to notice the goose bumps rising on Natalie's bare arms, but I'm having trouble looking away. Finally, for my own well-being, I shed my jacket and settle it over her shoulders.

She gives me a startled sideways glance.

"You looked cold," I say.

"Thanks." She bites her lip and pulls it closer around her.

When we get back to the dock, Natalie pays Rachel for

her Kegel balls and crams the pink box into her purse, and we walk back to the parking area together.

"This is me," Natalie says, pointing to a Honda Fit that has seen better days. "And hey, we're at least one-fifth of the way to me not getting fired."

"And me not landing my sister in the hospital again."

Natalie's curious gaze swings to my face. "Is that what happened last time?"

"When Quinn's letter got read for the will, yeah. It wasn't anyone's fault. She had preeclampsia. But the stress didn't do her any favors."

"That must have been scary."

I think about it again, the long wait in the hospital room, not knowing if Hanna or Eloise would be okay.

Natalie's watching me, interested and curious, and I almost tell her how much it fucking sucked, being afraid you weren't going to get a chance to fix things with your sister.

Instead, I say, gruffly, "You have my jacket."

She looks down at herself, like she'd forgotten it was there.

"Oh, yeah, sorry." She tugs it off and returns it to me.

When I get in the car, I throw it next to me on the passenger seat. But even at that distance, I can smell her cinnamon-apple scent the whole drive home.

The next night, I walk up the front path to my parents' house, bottle of wine in hand.

I'm still trying to sort out Preston's contradictions, to reconcile the asshole who tried to get me fired with the guy who clearly loves his sister enough to do anything for her. The guy who offered his suit jacket to me even though I hadn't let myself shiver with the guy who'd do pretty much anything to end a conversation with me.

The guy who looks like he could cow a roomful of C-suite executives into submission with the guy who blushes when you hand him a Fleshlight.

Though I've been trying hard *not* to think about Preston and that Fleshlight.

I ring the doorbell, and my mom answers—tall, slim, salt-and-pepper haired, beautiful in middle age, if a bit severe. "Natalie," she says. "Where's Lloyd?"

Right. On my own, I'm a disappointment. Story of my life.

"Hi, Mom. He—"

I almost say it. *He cheated on me, and I dumped his ass.* Or, you know, the mom-friendly version of that. But I can't quite bring myself to do it. My mom *loves* Lloyd. In her book, he's the best thing I've ever done—and when she found out he'd helped me make a plan to go back to school... Well. He could do no wrong, ever again.

"He's busy tonight."

"Oh," she says. "That's a shame. I love that boy. You know how much I love that boy."

"I do." I manage to swallow my sigh.

"Come in, come in," she says and ushers me into the dining room, where my sister and dad are already sitting at the table. I'm inside my on-time window, but like Mr. Fun, my parents are prompt, and if they told me dinner was at seven, they meant it.

That might be why I don't appreciate Preston's perspective on time management. It reminds me of how I grew up.

My parents' house is big, as befits a chief of surgery and a state supreme court justice, and well appointed. The kind of house where you can host dinner parties with important people. The five of us—my parents, my older sister, Jenna, and her husband, Marcus—are spaced too widely around a broad, elegant dining room table set with my mother's good china, dwarfed by the imposing dining room.

"Hi, Natalie," Jenna says, getting up and giving me a big hug. My sister smells faintly of something chemical, which makes sense because she's a big-shot biochemical engineer. She actually works with one of the Hott brothers, Quinn, at the lab he runs in Bend. I almost asked her to call in a favor with him when I applied for the Hott Springs Eternal job— but then decided not to. My sister has never made me feel as small as my parents do, but I don't want to be indebted to her for anything, either. I want my successes, when they finally come, to be my own.

My dad rises and gives me a hug. "Hi, Nat," he says.

I sit down and help myself to a spoonful of rice and some stew.

"Jenna was telling us about a breakthrough she made," my mom says proudly.

"I can't talk about the details yet," Jenna says, blushing, "but it was a good week."

"Yeah?" I say, cocking an eyebrow upward. "Congratulations."

"We're so proud of you, kiddo," my dad says.

I know it's not a zero-sum game—I *know* it's not—but it still hurts sometimes to hear them say that to her. Only because they've never, not once, said it to me.

"What *can* you tell us?" my mom asks, and Jenna launches into a complicated description of the properties of a certain molecule when it's supercooled.

Then it's Marcus's turn. He's the founder/CEO of a start-up that was recently acquired by a multinational conglomerate. He's been in Belgium working out the details, which will set up him and my sister for life. They could own a tiny house in every port.

My parents hang on his every word as he leads us through the series of ups and downs that resulted in his deal.

We're almost to dessert before my sister asks, "What have you been up to, Nat?"

I don't want to admit to myself how much I crave my family's—especially my mother's—approval, but the way my heart rate kicks up makes it hard to lie to myself. "I got a job," I say, then hate how much I sound like a little kid. So eager to please.

"What kind of job?" my mother says.

"Activities coordinator at Hott Springs Eternal. I'm developing a whole activities schedule for the resort."

My mother's mouth pinches. If you didn't know her as well as I do, you might not notice, but it's like a flag waving in my face. It's the patented Disappointed Face.

Once I asked my sister if she hated my mom's Disappointed Face as much as I did.

She said, *What disappointed face?*

I love my sister, but we grew up in the same household in parallel universes.

"Oh," my mother says. "What happened to that list I gave you, of careers in the medical field?"

"I'm not trained for any of that, Mom," I say. "That's why I have to go back to school."

"So why this job, then?" she asks. "I thought you were planning to go straight back to school?"

"That was never the plan," I say, keeping my voice calm with effort. "I don't have the money for it yet. I need to save up."

"Darling," she says, covering my hand with hers, "let us pay for school."

This again.

I cannot let my parents pay for school—for the same reason I can't come home to live with them. Because I can't stop feeling like they're waiting for me to fail.

One night when I was a senior in high school, I snuck

down to the kitchen for a midnight snack and overheard them talking in the kitchen.

My mom asked my dad, *What does having fun all the time equip you for?* and my dad said *Not much* and laughed.

I didn't know yet they were talking about me. Then my mom said, *It's like she was born completely without ambition,* and my dad said, *She's the one we'll have in our basement till she's fifty.*

That was the moment I vowed I would *never* move back home once I left. Or ask them for money, no matter how desperate I felt.

The thing is, sometimes I'm pretty sure they're right about me.

I went to college and got a communications degree. But I hated every job I got after that. I hated writing copy. I hated PR. I hated human resources.

Basically, I hated desks.

I don't know why I was surprised. I'd hated school. I loved being *at* school because I loved the people. But I hated sitting still and reading and writing. Getting paid for it didn't change that.

When you hate your job, your job has a tendency to hate you back.

I've been through a lot of jobs. And every time I leave one, I think about my parents.

She's the one we'll have in our basement till she's fifty.

When I got my first activities director position, at the nursing home, I freaking loved it. I thought my parents would be happy for me that I'd finally shown some ambition and turned being a people person and a perpetual partier into a potential career—but they were distracted and had bigger things to deal with. Like my sister's shiny career and my father's retirement party. My mom only said *I didn't know that was a job title* before losing interest.

And when the nursing home downsized and I got laid off, she said, *Well. It's an opportunity, really. For something better.*

Now I pull my hand out from under hers. "I want to pay for school myself."

"Admirable," my father says, in his judge's booming voice. There: decided and pronounced.

"You could go right away if you let us pay." My mother is working herself up to dig in.

Just then, my sister rescues me—although I don't think she does it on purpose. "Wait," she says, crossing her arms. "I figured something out. *You're* the one working with Preston. Oh my God! Oh, you *have* to hear this story," she tells my parents. "You know how Quinn had to do that thing where he worked as the receptionist at the spa? Because of his granddad's will? Well, all the brothers have to do something similar, and in Preston's case, he has to design a complete activities program for the resort, and he has to work with the resort's activities coordinator, and that's Natalie!"

"Wait, what's this?" my mom asks. "I thought *you* were designing the activities program."

"Right, I am, but, well—" God. "We have to work together for a few weeks till Preston fulfills the terms of the will. Then the job will be mine."

Assuming we pass the test.

The thought gives me an icy shiver, but I push the possibility of failure away.

"What does Lloyd think of the new job?" my mother asks.

"He thinks it's *great*," I say. "He's all for it."

She nods at that. "Okay. Well. It sounds like a good... first step."

Right. Now that it has Lloyd's stamp of approval.

It's going to suck when she finds out we broke up.

"And have you made a decision yet about which program you're applying to? I've been talking to people at work about the options and hearing good things about nursing administration."

I have to be honest, I haven't actually had time yet to look at the programs or to think about which one would be best for me. They all have names like *health information* and *medical records administration*, but when I look at them, they all look like *deskdeskdeskdesk*.

But there are loads and loads of careers in the medical field, and I'm sure there's something on the list that won't be like that. Something I'll like, that will offer me lots of earning and growth potential. That's the plan.

"Nursing administration is way up there," I tell her, and then I ask Marcus about the food in Belgium because it's so much easier when we're not talking about me.

12

NATALIE

A few days after dinner at my parents', I stand outside Hott Spot Spa and Salon and watch Preston amble toward me from the parking lot, the picture of casual male ease.

As he approaches, I take a moment to admire him again. How many summer suits does this guy *own*? Probably a lot, given that he works in finance in New York City. This one's camel-colored slub linen, and I want to touch it. You know, nothing inappropriate. A stroke over that right pec. Dusting away an invisible speck.

I sigh. Out loud.

"You okay?"

"Yeah, fine."

"Sonya meeting us?" he asks. Sonya is his brother Quinn's wife. Supposedly, they met because of some other wacky clause in Fox Hott's will.

"She said she might be a little late and that anyone could start us off with the tour and then she'd jump in to chat about programming possibilities."

As we reach the door, he steps ahead of me to open the door and holds it wide for me. I have to admit, as old-timey as the gesture is, I like it. I also like the whiff I catch of extremely expensive aftershave and, yeah, plain old Old Spice deodorant. Maybe I won't palm the suit. Maybe I'll nuzzle it instead, take a nice, deep breath. From briefly wearing his jacket over my shoulders, I know how good his scent is when concentrated.

Because sniffing my accidental coworker is an awesome idea.

The lobby of Hott Spot has the luxury-spa feel down to an art—big, airy, and decorated in neutral tones, with elegant but spare furnishings. Shelves line the walls, full of hair and body care products, but also bright-colored soaps, scarves, sponges, and other gifts. The space smells like flowers and baked goods, and soothing music pipes through carefully hidden speakers.

There are two women in the lobby. One, gray-haired and probably fifty-ish, sits behind the reception desk. The other is my height, weight, and—I'd guess—age, wearing a cute jumpsuit in a vivid floral. She's leaning on the desk in the manner of salon staffers everywhere whose clients are running late.

"Oh, here you are!" she says. "Come on back with me."

We're not late, of course, because we're following Preston's early-is-on-time rules. So I don't know why she sounds faintly aggravated with us, but I don't argue.

"I'm Brianna," she says as she leads us into a small treatment room. "And this is Amelia." She gestures to another woman, standing against a wall—tall, dark-haired, and smiling—who waves at us. "Anything we need to know before we get started?"

I'm startled that there are two of them—it seems like overkill for a spa tour—but I appreciate that Sonya's giving us the five-star treatment. "I don't think so?" I say. "Sonya said you'd get us started and then she'd take over."

"Oh, so you have an appointment with her afterward?"

I nod.

"Excellent," she says. "Then we should probably get started so we stay on track. You can keep your underwear on or take it off—and we're going to start with both of you face down on the tables, so slide in under the covers. I'll put you here"—she gestures at Preston—"and you here."

And then she and Amelia exit the room, leaving Preston and me open-mouthed and speechless.

13

PRESTON

"Wait, what?" I demand.

Natalie looks around at the empty room. For a second she looked as shell-shocked as I feel, then she lifts a shoulder and drops it.

"I guess this is Sonya's way to introduce us to the spa," she says. "Like the way Rachel demo'd the Wedding Night Launch for us."

"Like, we're supposed to…" I gesture at the tables. At us. "Get a couples massage?"

She seems to have completely recovered from the surprise. "I mean, you don't have to. You shouldn't if it makes you uncomfortable. But I don't want to be rude. If she set this up for us, I'm going to do it."

"I'm not getting couples massages with a woman I—"

I don't finish the sentence. I'm not even sure how I was *planning* to finish the sentence.

The amusement on Natalie's face hardens. "A woman you what? Hate?"

Startled, I stare at her. "I don't hate you."

Her eyebrows go up. "Coulda fooled me. You tried to fire me. You scowl and roll your eyes and glare. You flat-out told me my ideas suck. If you don't hate me, you probably should find a better way of showing it."

"I don't hate you," I repeat. I'm disturbed by the idea that she would think that—but yeah, I can see how she might. I sigh. "I owe you an apology. For trying to fire you."

She snorts. "Uh, *yeah.*"

"You didn't deserve that. There's no excuse."

"But you're going to tell me yours anyway?" It's her teasing voice again, and it's like fingertips over sensitive skin, raising goose bumps. I want to say, *Keep doing that. Just like that.* Or maybe even, *More. Harder.*

Instead, I answer the question. "I'm trying to get a deal inked at work, and it's a tricky one. Tense."

I'm not sure why I'm telling her any of this, but something about being alone in this quiet space has loosened tight knots in my throat and chest.

"That sucks," she says, and when I risk a glance at her, her expression is softer than I was expecting. "Is it a big deal? Like, important?" Her eyes rake over my face, curious.

"Yeah," I admit. "Maybe the most important thing I've ever done. The higher up you get in investment banking, the fewer career paths are open, and at the level I'm at, only a few people get to be managing director. I'm up for it, and so's another guy at work. Basically, which of us gets it comes down to which of us inks a deal first, and—well, the clock's ticking."

Her expression gets even softer. "And you're stuck here. With the will thing."

"And I'm stuck here," I agree.

She bites her lip, looking thoughtful. "That kind of sucks. And—" She hesitates. "Makes you make a lot more sense. Why you wouldn't want to work with me—because you think I'll slow you down. Why you're so brusque. Focused," she says. "Obsessed with efficiency."

They're not soft words. Or kind words. But they're not "grumpy asshole," either.

I guess neither of us hates the other.

There's a knock at the door.

Natalie starts, like she's forgotten where we are. "We need a couple more minutes," she calls.

"No rush," Brianna calls back.

Natalie looks at me. "Turn around," she orders. And she starts to lift her shirt.

Instinctively I turn—not because I don't want to see, but because I do, and I'm afraid of what will happen if I let myself.

I can hear fabric swishing over skin. The sound of clothes dropping onto the floor. The *shhh* as she settles herself against the table and as she pulls the top sheet over herself.

It's been a long time since I had a massage. I would like one.

I sigh. "Don't look," I say.

"Don't flatter yourself, Hott." She snickers. "God, that last name. The jokes write themselves."

"And there's not a new one under the sun," I say, laying my suit jacket over the chair. Stepping out of my shoes, pushing off my socks. Unbuckling my belt and slipping it out of the loops. My pants zipper sounds ridiculously loud in the quiet room.

I lie down on the table, wondering how I'm going to survive knowing that someone is touching Natalie's bare skin.

There's a quiet knock and Brianna and Amelia reenter, bustling around, adjusting the bolsters under our feet, the sheets over our backs, the headrests. They murmur quietly to each other. I hear the snick of the massage lotion pump and the squelch of the lotion on hands.

In a moment, I will hear the sound of that lotion brushing over Natalie's naked body in long, smooth strokes. The quiet hitch of pleasure in her breathing.

Something short-circuits in my brain.

I can't do this.

There's another knock at the door.

"Massage in progress," Brianna says over my back, in a low, unflustered voice.

The door opens a crack. "It's urgent," a voice says.

I recognize it as the receptionist's.

"Hang on a moment," Brianna says. "I'm so sorry."

There's a flurry of whispering at the door and then a flurry of murmuring between Brianna and Amelia, and then:

"Um, so this is awkward," Brianna says out loud. "You're not Ann Arnward and Paul Stevens."

Oh no.

"No," I say, resigning myself to the next round of humiliation. "We're Preston Hott and Natalie Archer. We're here to get a tour of the spa and meet with Sonya about partnering to bring some of your services to the resort as activities. Including couples massages."

"So, um, the thing is," Brianna says, "this appointment

was for Ann and Paul. And they've just showed up. There was a bit of confusion. Some communication...errors. We thought you were them."

Natalie starts giggling. "Oh my God," she says. "That's—I can't even—"

"I'm so sorry," Brianna says. "I thought you two were—"

"No, I'm so sorry!" Natalie says. "I thought Sonya told you to demo the couples massage for us!"

The massage therapists are laughing, too. Natalie has propped herself up on the bed to talk to Brianna, and I am definitely not looking at her bare arms and the topmost smooth, gorgeous curve of her tits.

And I'm struck again by how nothing fazes her. By how she's here, laughing through this mortifying moment...and how it doesn't feel quite as awful, because she thinks it's funny.

"We'll get dressed now," I tell Brianna and Amelia.

"You're good sports," Brianna says, patting me on the back. Then they slip out the door and close it behind them.

In the silence, Natalie giggles again. "Oh, my *God*," she says.

"I'll change first," I tell her.

It feels, somehow, safest, and right about now, it occurs to me that things might be a lot easier if I *did* hate her.

14

NATALIE

"I'm sorry again for the confusion," Sonya says again as she shows us around Hott Spot. We've all apologized several times for the mix-up. I left Amelia and Brianna big tips.

"It's a good story," I say. "I'm going to dine out on that for a long time."

I think about Preston taking off his clothes while I lay face down and tried not to picture what was happening out of my sight.

Who knew that the sound of a zipper descending was that...suggestive. That it could hint at so many other... visuals.

But whatever. On to the next step here.

Hott Spot is a great operation, and it's given us a bunch of new ideas beyond couples massage. Nail painting for kids. Lessons in beard trimming, bang cuts, and do-your-own eyebrows. Plus Sonya recently added yoga to the spa's offerings, and she can open a few extra slots to make some resort-exclusive workshops and classes.

"You want to see the hot springs?" Sonya asks.

"Yes!"

She leads us through the luxurious women's locker room and out onto the hot springs patio. The hot springs have been corralled into a stone-tile-edged pool. It's *beautiful* out here. There are rock outcroppings, a waterfall, a few small pools at different levels, and all kinds of amazing landscaping. Steam rises off the surface of the startlingly clear water. Somehow this space manages to capture both the exoticness and privacy of a jungle clearing as well as the high-end cache of a luxury spa. Not easy to do.

"God," I groan. "That water looks so tempting."

Preston shifts beside me. I know he said he doesn't hate me, but I'm still not sure. It seems like everything I do or say gets under his skin.

Sonya smiles at me. "You're welcome to use the spa any time you want after hours. Your employee keycard will get you in that gate." She shows me.

"Seriously?"

She grins. "Don't tell anyone. It's just family and friends."

My heart does a little *awww* at being included. Never mind that Sonya's the kind of big-hearted person who probably calls everyone a friend after an hour of hanging out.

"And here's a pro tip—there's almost *never* anyone here after nine p.m. No idea why, but it's basically deserted. Quinn and I like to come then." She blushes. "Maybe peek through the gate to make sure it's unoccupied before you enter."

I laugh. "Duly noted."

In some ways Sonya reminds me of my sister. She's got that whole glossy, polished thing going on—hair, nails, eyebrows, eyelashes, makeup. And her clothes are really nice—expensive looking and well fitting and probably designer. I'm betting she doesn't leave the house very often without looking in the mirror, which is a thing I accidentally do all the time. (Hello, salad greens in teeth.)

But Sonya is warm and friendly. She doesn't have the Teflon veneer of some beautiful women—including my mom and sister.

"There's no sulfur smell," I observe.

"No," Sonya says, smiling. "We're lucky. That smell is caused by bacteria that feed off sulfides, and this particular spring doesn't reach deep enough for that to happen." She tilts her head. "You two want a dip now? No one's in there. Pres, I've got some of Quinn's trunks in my office, and Nat, you could go in your—"

"*No,*" Preston says. "In fact, I'm on a call in five. Thanks for the tour and the ideas. We'll be in touch."

And he turns on one expensive dress shoe and strides away.

Sonya watches him go, an enigmatic expression on her face. She turns to me and raises her eyebrows. "How's it going with him?" she asks.

"About like that," I say, wincing. "Just when he seems to be softening toward me, he growls like a wolf with a thorn in its paw. I can't figure him out."

"But you're trying," she says, smiling.

"Yeah," I admit.

She smiles. "He's...an enigma." Her eyes move over my face, slowly, and then she seems to make a decision. "You won't be the first woman who came face-to-face with a Hott brother and needed some help figuring him out. You know he's not the first one to have to deal with their granddad's will, right?"

"There are a lot of rumors and stories."

She nods. "Yeah. Quinn's bit was having to work at the Hott Spot reception desk. And you haven't met Quinn yet, but that's like making Oscar the Grouch a greeter at a Michelin-starred New York restaurant."

I chuckle.

"And then Shane, who until recently was the picture in the dictionary next to *Hollywood fuckboy*, had to plan a celebrity wedding and somehow decided that the easiest way to pull that off was to be the groom in his own fake celebrity wedding."

"Seriously?"

"Yup."

"Their granddad is—"

"Sometimes we use the word *sadist*," she admits. "Hanna says it's more that he's a chess player and he's playing one half of a match the brothers don't know they're also playing—but I don't know. Jury's out. And we might never know, I guess. Since he's...gone."

"Wow," I say. "That's pretty intense."

She nods. "Yeah. I will say..." She hesitates, tipping her head to the side and eyeing me thoughtfully. "There's a bit of a pattern at this point. Of Hott brothers falling for the women they're paired up with in the will shenanigans. Quinn and me, Shane and his fake bride..."

I wave a hand. "Well. I'll *definitely* be the one who

breaks *that* pattern because there have *never* been two people less likely to end up together than Preston and me."

Even if, when I peeked and watched him retie his tie in the treatment room, I wanted to climb him like a tree.

"Yeah," Sonya says, dragging me back to the present, where I try not to blush furiously. "Preston is a tough nut to crack. Until a few days ago, I would have said Tucker was the 'toughest Hott to crack.' But Hanna has this client from New York who happened to mention that Preston's marriage imploded more than a year ago. Hanna didn't know. He hasn't told anyone, as far as we know, even though the divorce is inked and filed."

My mouth must have fallen open, because Sonya says, "Right? And the marriage was kind of a mystery to begin with. I never met her, but everyone says she was this flamboyant, super social SoHo artist."

I can't explain why the news of Preston's secret divorce hits me so hard. Why the idea of this uptight, arrogant, grumpy guy not wanting to tell anyone he got divorced gives me all the feels.

But I'm pretty sure Sonya can see right through me because her eyes move over my face again, curious and a little knowing. "This is how it starts," she says, and I think she's holding back a smile. "You start out wanting to understand what makes them tick."

"I don't—"

She grins and waves a hand. "It's okay," she says. "You tell yourself whatever you need to."

15

PRESTON

Today is pop-up rage-room day, and I'm—apprehensive.

The last couple of days have been, relatively speaking, uneventful. No sex toys, no nakedness—just a few meetings here and there with vendors. We talked to a company that does horseback rides, lasso lessons, and portable amusement park bull rides; then talked to the head of Wilder Adventures about setting up some rock climbs on the Hott land; then got a quick run-through from my brother-in-law, Easton, about whether the river that runs across the ranch would be better for rafting or paddleboarding (answer: the river's too lazy in that stretch for rafting, so paddleboarding). Natalie and I agreed to split up to do some research—her on Jell-O wrestling, body painting, and what it takes to put together a splatter room, and me on whether there's a music-booking company that could set up candlelight concerts.

None of those meetings or activities were hands-on. We

kept them brief and efficient and talked mostly to the vendors, not to each other.

In short, they felt safe.

But today Horace's Portable Madhouse is coming to HSE to demo the pop-up rage room, and Horace insists that the only way to truly experience the rage room is to get hands on.

I suggested that Natalie could experience it without me, but unfortunately Hanna was walking by us in the parking lot at exactly that moment. She turned a fierce scowl on me and said that *of all people* I could definitely stand to blow off some steam so there would be zero chance of my being an asshole again to her at any point during this pregnancy.

It wasn't an argument I was ready to have, so here we are.

It's an impressive operation, to be honest. Horace has erected a large tent and covered the ground with an absolutely enormous tarp. Privacy screens and mesh safety nets surround the rage space, and both of us are suited up with chest plates, thick gloves, clear face plates, and goggles.

We each have a baseball bat and a sledgehammer.

I feel ridiculous.

I'm not an angry guy. Grumpy, yeah, but not...angry.

It's pretty hard to imagine I'm going to get anything out of this.

We stand several feet apart, each facing our targets.

Natalie swings her baseball bat at an old VCR. Her first blow bounces off, and she giggles. She swings again, making better contact this time, and a piece of plastic flies off, the frame of the machine denting.

"Ha!" she says. "Take that!"

She attacks it again, with vigor, still laughing. We're both wearing long pants and long sleeves—rules of the room—yet even baggy overalls and a plain T-shirt can't keep her curves under wraps. I can't look away.

The baseball bat comes down. Hard. She kicks the platform the VCR sits on, and I almost say, *Be careful—you'll hurt your foot.* But then I see her face, and I realize:

She's definitely not laughing anymore.

She's *angry.* Grunting, swinging, flailing—yelling. She's yelling. "You *asshole!*" she yells. Her face is red.

And I'm standing and staring and watching her.

My chest is tight, and I realize...I'm angry, too. I'm pissed at whoever made Natalie feel like that. This is a woman who never loses her cool. Who laughs in the face of every ridiculous thing the world throws at her, and bounces back, looking for the fun factor. Something ugly must have happened to leave all that anger inside her, waiting to be unleashed.

I want to know what it is.

I might never know, and for some reason, that feels intolerable.

I take my sledgehammer to a nearby toilet. Just a tap at first. I work out several times a week—in fact, besides work, working out and running are basically the only other things I do in New York. I'm strong enough to wield the sledgehammer without a lot of difficulty. I raise it again and slam it down on the innocent toilet and—*crack.*

Jesus, that's satisfying.

And suddenly I get *angrier.* Like a *lot* angrier.

Kali could have told me how unhappy she was. She could have told me that she was looking at other men, that she was measuring them against me and liking what she saw. She could have told me that she knew it would be easy for her to fall for someone else because she wasn't getting what she needed from me.

Anytime, she could have said any of that, but she didn't.

Crack. It takes surprisingly little effort to reduce the toilet from a functional object to useless shards. And it feels shockingly good. Like I'm making something instead of destroying it.

Crack, crack, smash.

I look up to find Natalie watching me from where she stands a few feet away. My eyes meet hers. There's fire in hers. I can't look away from it. It's shocking and beautiful and primal. My body doesn't know if it's anger or something else; it only knows that she's amped up. And it wants to match her.

I want some of that.

Her pupils flare, like she feels the same.

My body tightens, a long line of lust. It would feel so good to unleash all the energy that's building in my body.

For the first time since she wrapped her hand around my tie, I let her see some of what I'm feeling. The need. The heat.

And she gives it right back. Our eyes stay locked, a circle of rising intensity, and my heart pounds. My breath is tight in my chest.

Horace's voice wafts into range. "You two all set?" he asks.

I guess he heard the silence and assumed we'd gotten our fill of smashing. And to be fair, he said most people do around five or ten minutes when they're demoing the room. Our time is probably well up.

I'm not done, though.

I'm definitely, definitely not done.

I want to shout, *Leave us alone*. But I don't. Of course I don't.

Natalie's gaze falls away from mine. She sets the baseball bat down. Her shoulders slump, like she's suddenly realized how tightly she's holding herself.

"Yeah," she calls back to Horace. "We're done."

16

NATALIE

What the hell *was* that eye-contact thing? It was...fierce. One minute I was raging at Lloyd, and then I turned to see Preston watching me with this dark hungry look, and my anger turned, on a dime, to something else. Something hot and needy and almost overwhelming.

I want to ask him: *Did that happen? Or was it some kind of anger-fueled delusion?*

And...*Will it happen again?*

Because that Preston, the passionate man barely holding his worst impulses in check...

I think I might want to know him better.

Of course I don't ask because Horace—wearing a T-shirt that says *Smashing Things Is Cheaper Than Therapy*—is now helping us out of our safety gear and telling us that there are lots of other things that can be smashed besides tech and toilets.

Instead, I ask Horace if he'd be willing to do a second demo at the Wilder-Hott party on Sunday.

At first, he's annoyed at the idea of having to demo himself twice, but when we explain the whole situation with the will—minus, once again, how Preston antagonized his sister—he agrees. Apparently he has some beef with Arthur Weggers, the lawyer who's been enforcing the will on Preston and his brothers, and he's more than happy to do whatever he can to cockblock him. His words, not mine.

As we leave the rage room, walking back toward the lodge, I half expect Preston to run away the second he has the chance. Instead, he asks, "Who is it?"

"Who is...?"

"When you were smashing the VCR. Who were you thinking about?"

"How do you know it's a *who*?" I ask, even though it totally, totally was. And then, "Who were *you* thinking of when you were smashing the toilet?"

He scowls and looks away. But I'm getting used to the scowls. I'm starting to understand they don't mean he doesn't want to talk.

"It's only fair," I point out. "If I tell you, you have to tell me."

"I asked first."

"It was a who," I admit. "It was my ex. He was having an emotional affair with his work wife."

He lets out a sharp hissing sound. Which is...satisfying.

"I shouldn't have been surprised. He was with her so much. It just hurt. Especially because he made it seem like I was the problem. That if I had more substance, if I wasn't just *fun*, maybe it would have worked out."

He shakes his head. "That's complete bullshit. He tried

to make it about you, but it was about him being a complete dickwad."

I'm quiet for a moment because, well, it's nice—hearing him say that. He's a guy who clearly never says anything he doesn't mean, so it has more weight, somehow.

"Thanks," I say finally, and he shrugs, like, *I didn't do much, but you're welcome.* "Even so, I never, ever want to be someone's fun-times girl again."

"Is that what he called you?"

His voice is tight. It reminds me of the heat in his eyes right before Horace interrupted.

"It's what I was to him."

It's quiet for a moment, only the sound of our footsteps as we walk.

"What was his name?" he asks.

"Lloyd."

"Lloyd," he repeats, squinting.

That makes me laugh. "Worst name ever, right? It's like that scene in *When Harry Met Sally* when he's all, 'A Sheldon can do your income taxes. If you need a root canal, Sheldon's your man...but humpin' and pumpin' is not Sheldon's strong suit.'"

There's another long silence, and I think maybe I've shocked him. Until he says, "Was it Lloyd's strong suit?"

"I mean, it wasn't *bad*," I say.

"That," he says, the corner of his mouth turning up, "is pretty damning."

Is he *smiling*? "It is, kind of, isn't it?"

"If that was the best thing anyone could say about me in bed? I'd move to Siberia and swear off sex."

I snort.

"God, I hope no one has *ever* said that about sex with me," he says fervently.

I'm guessing no one has ever said sex with Preston "wasn't bad." Because he can look at a woman like she's, God, I don't even know, *dinner*—and he has so much intensity and focus, like if he decided you were what he was doing, he would *do* you absolutely as well as he knew how to—

This is not a productive line of thought.

"Who was yours?"

"My...?" He's confused, and I let myself wonder what *he* was thinking about, what caused him to lose the thread of the conversation.

"Who you thought of while you smashed that toilet."

"Oh," he says. "Right."

"You said you'd tell."

"I didn't technically say I'd tell—"

"You implicitly agreed by saying you asked first and pushing me to tell you after we'd discussed the fact that it was only fair for you to tell if I told."

"Whoaaaa," he says, and holy shit, he's definitely smiling. And it's so...*pretty*. Eye crinkles and dimples and straight white teeth. Everything about him gets brighter, and—

I want to do it again. I want to make him smile again.

"You ever thought about law?" he asks.

"Never once," I say, and he does—he smiles, and we're walking side by side, like maybe we're friends or something.

"Don't think I'm going to let you off the hook," I warn.

He's quiet, and I think he's not going to tell me. And I

wouldn't be surprised. This is Preston, after all. He has not become a titan of New York finance by showing his cards.

"Kali," he says abruptly. "My ex-wife. She asked me for a divorce about a year ago. She'd met someone else, and she wanted to—to see where it went."

And holy shit. He told me something I know he hasn't even told his family. Preston Hott doesn't open up easily, and he's given me something he's been holding incredibly close to his chest.

"I'm sorry," I say quietly.

His gaze flicks over to me. There's grief in it. He's letting me see it. "You get it," he says.

There are so many things I could say, but I settle on the only one that seems like it might help.

"I do."

That's it. That's the whole conversation. Right then we reach the lodge, and he says he needs to check in about something at the front desk, and I head to the elevator.

But as we part ways, my chest is a whole village of warm fuzzies.

17

———————

NATALIE

"This is so fun!" Rachel tells me, sweeping an arm out to encompass all the festivities at the Wilder-Hott party, which includes not only Wilders and Hott and their significant others and kids, but also what appears to be hundreds of friends. "I can't believe you guys put all this together in a week."

"We have good partners," I tell her, giving her an affectionate side hug. She hugs me back.

All the Wilders and Hotts are doing their demos for free today. When Hanna told me that, I got teary. Yes, technically Sonya and her staff work for Hanna, but Hanna says she offered them pay and they wouldn't take it. Neither would Gabe, Rachel, or Brody, all of whom are volunteering today because they love Hanna and want her to succeed.

Yeah, Hanna said, her eyes suspiciously shiny, when I told her how amazing I thought that was. *They're pretty great.*

Rachel's demo is quiet for the moment. She's hosting a

wine tasting, and Brody is doing nature talks (reinterpreted for Hanna's backyard), with a few of their staffers periodically relieving them so they can take breaks and experience the other activities. A short distance away, Sonya's coworkers are hard at work: Brianna and Amelia are offering chair massages, a woman I was introduced to as Reggie is painting nails, and someone I haven't yet met is teaching yoga.

Gabe Wilder, one of Hanna's brothers-in-law, is teaching kids to boulder on an immense craggy rock with a thick pad below, and a sign directs partygoers down to the river if they're interested in doing some paddleboarding with Easton. That's been one of our biggest hits, along with horseback rides and lasso lessons.

Of course, Horace's Portable Madhouse is an even bigger hit...

But Jell-O wrestling has had the longest line all afternoon.

I wander away from Rachel and sidle alongside Preston. "Told you so," I tell him, because I can't resist crowing. "Everyone loves Jell-O wrestling."

He scowls at me, but I can see his heart's not in it. He surveys what we created with something soft in his expression that makes me think he's pleased.

"It's so...dumb," he says, but there's no heat in it.

"I think you mean it's so *fun*."

"I meant what I said," he tells me, giving me a stern look that I don't actually hate at all.

"We did it," I say. "We met our first milestone."

He crosses his arms across his broad chest and scowls deeper. "We're nowhere near done. I'd guess we have, what, less than half of the activities we need by the time the summer festival rolls around? And we've picked the low-hanging fruit."

"We've got this," I say, shrugging. "Ye of little faith."

Ever since the rage room, it's been more like this. Our combativeness feels different now, like we're somehow on the same side.

It feels good, and also...dangerous. Like I knew what to do with Preston when I thought he hated me, or at least was holding me at arm's length. This Preston—one I nudge with my shoulder, almost affectionately—is too big, too beautiful, and too likable.

It doesn't help that he's wearing cutoff navy sweats and a gray T-shirt. Stripped of his armoring suits, he seems younger and more vulnerable. Not to mention that the soft cotton loves his muscular body.

As, we already know, do I.

I tear my gaze from the intersection of T-shirt sleeve and curved bicep.

"I love your family," I tell him. I point to where Quinn and Shane are demolishing each other in the Jell-O pit while a horde of Wilder children cheer on one or the other. "They seem like they're all good people."

His expression softens. "I don't know the Wilders well, but they all jumped in to help Sonya and Quinn when there was a flood at Hott Spot last year. And my brothers...they can be grumpy bastards, but Quinn and Shane, when they got their letters from Granddad, they totally stepped up. And earlier this summer, Hanna was trying to host a celebrity wedding—January Stark and Tobias Bauer—"

"Tobuary!" I say delightedly, because like everyone else on Earth, I shipped January and Tobias. Hard.

"Someone tried—well, we *think maybe* they tried—to sabotage it, and all my brothers came through to—"

He's cut off by Hanna. "Pres!" she says, racing up to his side. "I need to finish frosting a cake, and I just heard Eloise waking up over the monitor, and Easton's down at the river. Any chance you could grab her for me?"

"On it," Preston says and strides off.

I watch him go, stunned.

Hanna is already trotting back toward the house.

"Hey!" I call.

She turns back.

"Can I help with the cake?"

She shrugs. "You ever frosted a cake? Because I haven't."

"No, but I'm game to try."

She grins, giving me a sec to catch up. "You know what I like about you?" she says as we hurry to the house together. "I actually believe that's true."

WHEN WE'RE DONE FROSTING the cake, Hanna starts making caramel glaze for the apple pie, and Rachel offers to introduce me to anyone I haven't met yet. We head back out into the grassy yard, which stretches for a good distance and is surrounded by a wooden lattice fence with a swinging gate. Beyond it, I can see the spa, which means that Hanna can basically roll out of bed and into the springs.

Not too shabby. Yet another good reason for Hanna's

brothers to fight like hell to hang on to the land for their sister.

Rachel and I weave among the activities as she introduces me to, or at least points out, her sisters-in-law and sisters-in-law-to-be. "Most of my brothers-in-law are in line for either Jell-O wrestling or nail painting right now," she says, laughing and pointing out the Wilder men in her life one by one and then moving on to Hanna's brothers, Rhys—who's in town only for the day—Tucker, and Quinn. She gestures toward Shane, the fifth brother, who's standing next to his fiancée, Ivy, the two of them looking like they're alone in their own happy world. Then she tells me the kids' names and who they belong to—Justin to her and Brody, and the rest to various Wilder brothers and their wives.

Everyone's talking and laughing, hugging and trying to draw each other into activities. This is the kind of family I always imagined myself with—fun and games, everyone enjoying themselves fully.

It's almost like Preston and I were swapped at birth.

My head is overflowing with names, spinning, by the time we get back to Sonya, who's taking a break from supervising her staff to eat. "I know you know Sonya," Rachel says. She turns to her. "We had such a hilarious moment on the boat the other day. I had everything prepared for Hanna and Natalie, and then Nat showed up with Preston, and I didn't have the brains to do a complete pivot, so I went with it. With poor Preston playing the unsuspecting groom."

"Oh, God!" Sonya says, turning to me with huge eyes. "That must have been hilarious." She claps her hand over her mouth. "Oh no, and then you came to the spa and—

you poor things!" She addresses Rachel again. "There was a mix-up. The front desk accidentally sent them into a couples massage appointment."

"Are you serious?!" Rachel says. "I wish I'd been a fly on the wall for that."

Both women are giggling uncontrollably. Sonya bites her lip. "I hope your luck looked up after those two days," she says.

I think of the rage room and almost tell them about the strange moment that passed between Preston and me—and the confessions that followed—but before I can, my attention is diverted by the sight of Preston walking toward us, a toddler on his hip. He's deep in conversation with her about something.

As they get closer, I realize he's not talking to her at all. He's holding a stuffed cat, monologuing in a squeaky Southern drawl interspersed with dramatic meows, pretending to be the voice of the toy. The toddler, who looks to be somewhere around a year to eighteen months old, holds a stuffed dog and is woofing back at him.

I'm completely charmed.

"Mr. Dog, sir, I know you want to be seated absolutely right away, but we simply do not have anything open at the moment. You'll have to wait your—"

The toddler holds the dog up to his face and woofs urgently.

"Sorry, El," he says, kissing her on the nose. "Mr. Dog, sir, you'll have to wait your turn."

"Woof, woof," the toddler says as Preston clocks the three of us standing and watching.

"This is Hanna's daughter, Eloise," Sonya says. "Want me to take her?" she asks Preston.

"Nah, we're good—right, El?" he says. "El, say hi to my friend Natalie." He nods toward me, something wry on his lips.

The word "friend" absolutely shouldn't give me a tiny thrill.

"Ha!" Eloise says.

"Hi, Eloise," I say back.

"Preston!"

The cry comes from behind us. Hanna, calling out the back sliders. "I don't know what I did to the caramel—"

Preston turns to scowl at his sister. "Oh, Jesus, Hanna, caramel? You can barely work the microwave, but you had to prep something notoriously impossible for an enormous party?"

"Can you help?"

He rolls his eyes. "Yes, of course. Coming." He pauses, looking down at his niece. "Actually..." he says to Sonya.

She laughs. "Yup." She opens her arms and takes Eloise and the stuffed dog, then reaches for the stuffed cat. Eloise pokes out a pudgy hand and shoves the cat back toward her uncle.

"You want Uncle Preston to keep Saucy Cat?" he asks her earnestly.

She nods.

Preston starts toward the house, tucking Saucy Cat into his pocket, and Eloise opens her mouth and howls.

He turns back. "You want to keep Saucy Cat," he guesses. Eloise brightens, and he hands her the cat.

But when he turns to go again, Eloise bursts into tears.

"Hey, kiddo!" Rachel says to Eloise. "He'll be back."

But there's no convincing Eloise of that fact. Her howl intensifies, tears streaming down her face, both her hands reaching for her uncle's receding back.

"We're going to have to follow Uncle Preston, aren't we," Sonya says.

Eloise's tears dry up, and she nods.

"Sorry," Sonya says to me. "Can we get together soon?"

"Definitely," I tell her, and she and Eloise follow Uncle Preston into the kitchen.

I watch them go, filled with sympathy for Eloise. I know exactly how it feels to want more of Preston's time and attention.

18

PRESTON

Natalie was right. About pretty much everything.

Watching my four big, tough brothers—and five even bigger, even tougher Wilder brothers—get their nails painted has been an unexpected treat.

Brawny, bearded Gabe Wilder's nails are ten different shades of pink, including four with glitter.

I didn't even know there were that many shades of pink.

Horseback riding, lasso lessons, the rage room—they're all huge hits.

And apparently people love submerging themselves in an enormous kiddie pool of Jell-O with other people and rolling around. Go figure. There's no accounting for taste.

I look around for Natalie. She's astride a horse, walking it around the perimeter of Hanna's enormous back yard, under the instruction of a tall, broad-shouldered twentysomething in a cowboy hat. Her tits bounce with the horse's motion—a glorious sight to behold—but that's not the thing that makes it impossible to look away. It's the expression on her face. She's beaming, delighted.

I'm not the only person who's noticed. The cowboy at her side can't take his eyes off her, either. And I'm pretty sure it's not her smile that has his attention.

My hands clench into fists.

"She's pretty good at her job, huh?" Shane asks. I turn to find him at my side, also watching Natalie. It's hard not to because joy radiates off her, like sunlight. There's an intense magnetism to how much she's enjoying herself. Or maybe that's just me.

I want to be closer to her.

"It's lucky that you're not trying to fulfill the terms of Granddad's will on your own," another dry voice says. "You'd be totally screwed."

"Look who's talking, Quinn," I growl. "Best receptionist Hott Spot's ever had."

Both my brothers are wearing swim trunks and T-shirts and are soaking wet from the garden hose. Even so, they have leftover bits of purple Jell-O still clinging to their clothes, hair, and bodies.

"She's easy on the eyes, too," Shane muses aloud, looking from me to Natalie.

"Don't be a dick, Shane," I growl.

Quinn shrugs one shoulder. "Don't let him goad you."

"Who's goading anyone?" I say, trying for an equally careless shrug and failing miserably. "I'm not interested in her."

Quinn winces. "You don't want to go there, dude. It's like catnip to him." He tilts his head at our brother.

When Quinn told Shane he wasn't interested in Sonya, Shane went to town messing with Quinn's head. Of course, now Shane's planning his own wedding, and he's so gone for Ivy that I can't imagine him playing those kinds of games.

"It's not like that," I say. "Natalie's not my type. We couldn't be more different."

Both my brothers eye me suspiciously.

I throw my hands up. "What?"

"We're not saying you're interested," Quinn says carefully. "It's just that, well, Grandfather's plans have a way of working out."

"Quinn and Sonya couldn't be more different, either," Shane says. "On paper. And look at Ivy and me. Small-town girl; bright-lights, big-city guy. Fame avoider, fame seeker."

"Yeah, well, not gonna happen this time."

I make myself look away from the sight of Natalie's deliciously thick thighs locked around the horse's flanks.

I am not fucking jealous of a horse.

Except I'm looking back. Again. Imagining those thighs—

She's done with her lesson. She dismounts, gives the cowboy a hug...

"Not interested, huh?" Shane says, looking down at my hands, clenched so tight my knuckles are white.

I close my eyes.

"So..." he says quietly, suddenly serious—and I should scent trouble because Shane's rarely serious. "Were you ever going to tell us about your divorce?"

"No," I admit. Then, "How'd you find out?"

He shrugs. "Hanna has a client from New York. I guess it's not as well-kept a secret as you thought."

"I wasn't trying to keep it a secret," I say.

"Only from us?" Shane asks. He doesn't sound as hurt

or angry as he probably deserves to be. "Did you think we'd give you shit about it?"

The truth is I didn't want to talk about it. Especially not with people who know the history. I still don't. But they're both waiting for an answer.

A hand touches my arm. "Hey," Natalie says. And I can't help any of the things that happen next—not the unclenching of my fists or the unclenching of the tightness in my chest. I'm really fucking glad to see her, so much that it surprises me.

She looks from my brothers to me and back again, and for a moment I'm terrified that she's going to apologize for interrupting and leave us alone again, so I'll have to answer Shane's question. But she doesn't. She turns to the two of them, holds out her hand, and says, "Hi! I'm Natalie. I don't think we've met."

My brothers introduce themselves, and Natalie asks them what their favorite activities have been so far.

"Definitely the Jell-O pit," Shane says.

Natalie raises both her eyebrows at me.

"Just because my brother's a caveman..." I say.

"Don't knock it if you haven't tried it," Natalie teases.

"You haven't tried the Jell-O pit?" Shane says. "Have you *ever* done Jell-O wrestling?"

"Nope," I say.

"Now's your chance!" Natalie says buoyantly. "Shane, you and Preston should wrestle."

"No way," I say.

"Oh, come on," Quinn says. "Even I did it. It's pretty fun."

All three of them face me, arms crossed.

"I mean," Natalie says, "if you're going to bring an activity to *your sister's resort*, you should probably vet it first, right? Make sure it's safe?"

I glare at her, but it's clear I've lost this one. Besides, she did save me from the third degree by my brothers. So maybe I owe her this win.

Also?

Pretty sure I can take Shane.

"Okay," I concede and turn to face my brother. "You're on."

19

____

PRESTON

Shane, Natalie, and I stand in line, waiting for my turn in the Jell-O pit.

"Good thing you didn't wear a suit," Natalie says, eyeing me up and down in a way that I like way more than I should.

"If I were wearing a suit, no way would I agree to this," I say.

I'm wearing cutoff sweats and a T-shirt—clothes I can stand to sacrifice to the god of purple Jell-O.

Natalie is wearing a pair of capri leggings and another of her tunic tops, this one a tank. Her arms are luscious, bare expanses of satiny skin. I can't look too directly at them, or I start to think about what that skin would feel like under my tongue. What the rest of her would feel like.

"Next," Kane Wilder—Jell-O pit supervisor—says. Natalie gives me a shove in the small of my back, and I step forward.

"Who's your opponent?"

"I am," Shane says, stepping forward next to me.

By this point, the pool has largely lost its audience because all the kids have moved on to playing some kind of mammoth game of capture the flag, the older kids keeping the younger ones in line. And I'm grateful for that at least.

"Oh, this should be good."

I turn to see Hanna standing next to Quinn and Natalie.

"I put my money on Shane. He has a personal trainer," Hanna says. "And this guy"—she gestures at me—"he's got a desk job."

She's grinning, and I'm feeling pretty good about actually doing something that makes my sister happy instead of angry and miserable.

"Shit," Shane says suddenly, reaching for his phone in his pocket. "I have to take this. Natalie," he says, "will you take over for me? You're my champion. Your victory is my victory. Tickets to my next premiere if you win."

What? What fresh hell is this? I glare at my brother, then turn the glare on Natalie, willing her to refuse. Not because I don't want to have my hands all over her in a pool of Jell-O. I do. Way too much.

It's exactly the sort of situation I should avoid with her. Like playing with sex toys and getting a couples massage and smashing things.

I'm batting a thousand.

Natalie doesn't refuse. Instead, she beams at Shane. "Of *course*," she says. "I would kill for those tickets. Wrestling your brother into submission should be a piece of cake and would be my great honor."

Wrestling your brother into submission.

That should not be sexy.

And yet blood has reversed itself from key locations *like*

my fucking brain and reoriented itself to where I definitely don't need any more of it.

"Don't let him wimp out," Shane instructs Quinn and Hanna, then swipes his phone and jogs off, saying "Ernst? What's up?"

"Oh, don't worry," Hanna says darkly. "No *way* he's wimping out. He owes me some good entertainment."

They're seriously going to watch me Jell-O wrestle my hot coworker. That's—

Probably illegal in several states.

Kane Wilder has been watching and listening with more amusement than I think is warranted. Now he says, "Okay, people, let's keep this moving. Lots of demand for the Jell-O pool. Hop in."

Kane helps Natalie into the pool. She stands in the middle of the purple mess, grinning at me, and fuck me if I can't marshal any resources to refuse.

"Preston," Hanna says sternly, and Quinn takes a menacing step toward me. Aside from Tucker, who could fell a giant with his left hand, Quinn is my biggest brother and probably has fifty pounds of sheer muscle on me. I quickly step into the pool.

Natalie gives me a tentative shove. The Jell-O underfoot is way more slippery than I was expecting, and it takes me a second to find my footing. I give her a tentative shove back.

She's smiling.

"Why are you smiling?" I ask.

"Because I know something you don't know."

It's a line from *The Princess Bride*, which I've watched more times than—than I care to admit.

"What's that?" I ask.

"I played women's club rugby for years," she grunts, and then, before I can prepare myself, she lowers her shoulder, wedges it against my thigh, and shoves, surprisingly hard. And even though I must have fifty pounds on her, she's strong and she's currently much lower to the ground. I go back onto my ass, and Natalie, who may have put more power into the move than was strictly necessary, lands on top of me.

I smirk at her.

"Why are you giving me that smirky face?" she asks.

"Because I know something you don't know."

"What's that?" she asks.

"I was on the high school wrestling team."

I neatly flip her, pinning her beneath me. And we're both laughing, our faces inches apart, and it feels so fucking good to laugh with her—

And then we're not laughing. Because she's all generous curves, but beneath the softness is surprising strength, and she's fighting to get her advantage back, writhing under me, flexing against me, and—

Fuck.

It feels good and her gaze locks on mine and neither of us looks away and—

"Time!" Kane calls, and suddenly I remember that we're in a giant kiddie pool of purple Jell-O, that we're at a family party, and that my sister and brother are standing over us watching.

The world rushes back, and I scramble off her, trying to figure out if I stand up how obvious my arousal will be. I catch her eye, and she bites her lip like she knows, moving to stand between me and our audience. Which...I mean, it helps with one problem, but now she's standing there, her delectable heart-shaped ass inches from my—

Bond price formula!

Price = (Coupon × (1-(1+r)^-n)/r) + Par Value/(1+r)^n

It takes a few times through, but it works like a charm.

I'm able to accept the congratulations of my family members without ruining the whole party's good time.

20

———

NATALIE

s dusk turns to dark that night, I lower myself into the Hott Spot springs with a groan of pleasure.

Celebration time.

Yes, we have a long way to go. But today went incredibly well, and there's every reason to believe we're going to meet the terms of the will, get the Hott Springs Eternal activities program off to a strong start, *and* return Preston to New York in time to meet his ridiculous deadline.

I deserve a long, hot soak.

Plus I need time to think about things.

Like what happened in the Jell-O pool.

I should never have taken Shane's place. I guess I got caught up in the moment. Everyone was having fun. It all seemed harmless.

Lesson learned: It's all fun and games until someone gets poked in the thigh by Preston Hott's big, hard cock.

All of a sudden, I was wanting things I had no right to

want. I imagined opening my arms and spreading my legs and letting his weight pin me to the ground. I wanted—

God, I *wanted*.

I still want.

And, if the...sturdiness of his arousal was any indication, I am apparently not the only one.

"Hey," a voice says from the gate.

A deep voice, slightly roughened from a long day, rasps over my overheated, oversensitive skin like the stroke of a calloused hand.

"You, um, mind company?" Preston asks.

I shake my head.

"I came down for a soak, but if you'd rather—I don't want to intrude."

"You're not intruding. There's plenty of room for both of us."

I'm not sure that's true. There might not be enough room in the world for the two of us and my body's reaction to him.

He sets his towel on a table, then pulls his T-shirt over his head. It's almost completely dark out now, except for small landscaping lights and the fairy lights that ring the enchanted space, but I can see well enough. And all the breath leaves my body, because he's beautiful. *Renaissance statue* beautiful, *romance novel cover* beautiful. Sculpted pecs, ridged abs, sturdy shoulders, and God's gift to arms.

He slides into the springs, and my nipples tighten at the sight of him and the tease of the rippling water.

He sits a couple of feet away from me. A theoretically safe distance. And he submerges himself to his chin under the surface of the water, which lets me draw a few full breaths.

"It was really nice to meet your family," I say.

"Thanks."

"You and your brothers—you seem to really love each other. Despite the shit they give you."

"Yeah," he says. "Hey. Thanks for, um, saving me from the third degree with Shane and Quinn."

"They were asking you about Kali, huh?"

He nods. "I didn't want to talk about it with them."

"You probably don't want to talk about it with me, either, then," I say lightly. Because I want to know, but I don't want to force him.

But he shakes his head. Shrugs. And—I don't think it's my imagination—moves closer to me along the ledge submerged beneath the steaming surface of the water.

"I met her at college," he says.

My pulse kicks up. He's confiding in me, and I want to take his words and tuck them into a treasure box and keep them safe.

"My granddad—" He stops.

"You and your siblings all were raised by your grandfather?"

"My mom and a series of husbands—we have three different dads, which is why we don't all look alike—but yeah, my grandfather was this kind of—I don't know. Patriarch? Titan? He was always there for us, but he was also..." He hesitates. "Always an asshole. Had to be right. Had to win. Knew what was best."

"That sucks," I say because—sometimes that's all you *can* say. And I worry for a second that it's wrong, but he nods, and the corner of his mouth curves—his not-quite-smile.

Someone who didn't know him might not even catch it as it flits by. But I know him.

"He didn't want me to go to college on the East Coast. We got into a pissing match about it, and I dug in. He's a stubborn son of a bitch, and…" He stops again.

"And so are you?"

His eyes flash to mine, the corner of his mouth curving higher. "Yeah. So I went. Studied finance because I thought it would help me when I went home to run the ranch. Except I fell in love with Kali."

His voice is low. Rough. Vulnerable. I'm peeking into the heart of this gruff, self-contained man, and my own heart constricts at the gift of it.

My heart's pounding. I think of Sonya saying *This is how it starts. You start out wanting to understand what makes them tick.*

Now I want to ask her, *And then what? What happens once you find out what makes them tick?*

"I came home with her, and he—he *hated* her."

"Because—"

"He was already angry at me for leaving. And Kali's dream life was in New York, and that's where she wanted us to live. But also, she was an artist and a social butterfly, which were two things he couldn't understand at all. He said if I went to New York with her it would end badly. He threatened to disinherit me if I did. We got into a huge fight. He said I wasn't cut out for New York finance, that it would eat me alive. That I'd regret leaving the one thing I was actually good at. That I'd end up back in Rush Creek, begging to run the ranch."

I wince.

"Yeah. It was ugly."

"You've proved him wrong," I tell him.

I want to say, *You don't have to keep proving yourself.* But I don't want to make him shut down, either. I want more of this. More Preston.

"Not yet," he says. "But when I get this promotion, I will have."

"Why that?"

"Because everything else I've done, a lot of people do. But this promotion I want—not a lot of people ever get this far. It's rarefied air. This is the hard part."

This. This is what makes Preston Hott tick. This is why he was so angry at getting called back here, why he was so combative that he tried to have me fired. Why it's been so hard for him to comply with the will. Because to him, it still feels like his grandfather is trying to take away what's important to him.

He sighs heavily.

"You okay?" I ask.

"Yeah," he says. "Feels, um, good to talk about it."

"Thanks for telling me."

"Yeah. Of course."

But we both know there's no *of course* about it.

"It went well today," he says, and I know if he wants to talk about activities planning, he must *really* want to change the subject. It makes me smile.

"It did."

"People seemed like they were having fun."

"Did you have fun?" I ask him.

Creases form between his eyebrows.

"That's not supposed to be a hard question," I say, laughing.

He looks away. "I don't know if I know how to have fun."

Oh, Preston. But that makes sense, too.

"What about when you were a kid?" I ask.

He runs his hand over the surface of the water, and his fingers nearly brush me. I've been moving closer to him all this time, drawn in by his story. "What about it?"

"Did you have fun then?"

"Someone had to watch out for Hanna," he says. "Someone had to make sure Shane and Quinn didn't kill each other. Someone had to call 911 when Tucker decided it would be a good idea to try to jump from one tree to another like Tarzan."

So he could never let down his guard. Never be a kid. My chest tightens. "So, basically, you were the grown-up."

"I guess I never thought about it like that—but yeah, kind of. Not when we were really little. Back in those days, we played capture the flag and tag and all those kinds of games. And yeah. It was fun. We'd run and play, and there was so much space and so many hours before we'd get called to dinner."

He's got a faraway look in his dark eyes, staring at memories over my shoulder. A smile tugs at both corners of his mouth now, and I have to make myself stop staring at how beautiful it makes his chiseled face. At some point, he's drifted even closer to me. I'm breathless.

His eyes snap back to my face. "We made a pact," he says abruptly. "The five of us brothers. That when we all grew up, we'd stay or come back, and run the ranch together." He holds out his hand to show me a scar at the base of his thumb. "We swore a blood oath."

I reach for his hand. He lets me cradle the back of his hand against my palm. The heat of his skin singes me, in the best possible way.

"And you—"

"And I broke it. We all broke it. But I was the first one."

I haven't known him long, but even I understand that when he broke that oath, something in him broke, too. I ache for him.

I can't help myself; I run a fingertip over his wet skin along the scar, and it's like touching a live wire. For him, too, I think because he rasps out something between a sharp exhale and a grunt. My breath catches, a quieter echo.

My eyes find his, dark and frank and pleading, and I can't look away.

His gaze drops to my mouth.

"Preston," I murmur, and my voice doesn't even sound like mine. "Maybe you need to do something just for fun."

"Maybe I do," he murmurs back, right before he takes another step closer and his mouth comes down, hard, on mine.

She whimpers and clutches me. Her mouth opens, instantly generous, and God, her lips are so fucking soft. Her tongue slips against mine, silky and welcoming. Hunger flashes through me. I'm raw and ravenous, the kiss greedy and slick and combative. Like we're fighting for control, even in this.

"Natalie," I groan as she glides closer. She's wearing a bikini, and she's all smooth wet skin, slick against mine, and it's driving me crazy. Lighting me on fire. I touch her waist, and it's just like I thought, satin and squeezable, and I want more of her, I want my hands all over her, I want my mouth all over her.

For now I content myself with loving how her bare skin tightens with goose bumps under my touch. I content myself with running one hand up the perfect, pretty slope of her belly until I find what I've been fantasizing about, the weight of her breast in my hand. I explore all the curves that she offers to me—the sensitive underside, the generous roundness. And then my fingertips brush over her hard nipple, and she whimpers and clutches me, hungry and trusting. It almost undoes me, but it also makes me remember that she's vulnerable.

So, reluctantly, I drop my hand and break the kiss. I force myself to put distance between us.

"Preston."

My name is a question.

"I want—" I start, but I can't even finish the sentence. There are too many things. I want to pinch that peaked nipple, roll it, tease the tip until her knees go weak. I want to find out how to make her come, if I can bring her there with my mouth on her breasts and my fingertips on her clit, or if she needs more. My thigh between hers. My mouth between her legs. My fingers crooked inside her.

My cock.

"God, Natalie" is all I can manage.

"Then *take* it," she says. "Take what you want."

Holy fucking God. This woman.

But I take a deep breath. Drop a kiss onto her forehead.

"It's not fair to you," I say. Instead of devouring her, instead of tasting every inch of skin. "It wasn't fair of me to kiss you like that when you *told* me you never want to be someone else's fun-times girl ever again. And then I went and did exactly what you said you didn't want."

"What if I changed my mind?" she whispers.

"But you haven't, have you?" I ask.

Slowly she moves away from me. The glazed look leaves her eyes, and her shoulders sag. She says, "It just sucked. What happened with Lloyd."

"Yeah," I say.

"To know he'd slotted me in that way. So I was just good

times and good in bed, and she was—everything real to him."

I hope I never meet this guy because I will pulverize him and end up in prison.

"He was a spectacular idiot," I tell her. "If he couldn't see all the things that are amazing about you. I think you're—"

"Don't say 'great,'" she warns, and there's a tease in her voice now. I'm glad to hear it because for a second I was worried I'd ruined everything—whatever tentative friendship we'd forged, our working relationship. "And quit flattering yourself that I want anything more from you than fun, either, Mr. Tie's-So-Tight-I-Can't-Breathe."

She scoots away from me, leaning against the edge of the pool. It's smart of her and the right thing for both of us —her putting that extra distance between us.

And also, shit, she's right. What an arrogant son of a bitch I am to have made her into the needy one when *I* kissed *her*. When I took what I wanted, even though I didn't have much to give. "God," I say. "I'm a dick. I know I'm no prize. If the events of the last two years have taught me anything, it's that."

"No," she says. "I'm sorry. I didn't mean to strike a nerve. She gave you shit about that? About being—"

"Uptight? A workaholic? Inaccessible? Rigid?"

She flinches.

"Maybe not exactly those words," I say. "But yeah."

"What's she like?"

"An artist. She lives big. Bright. Lots of colors and people around her. Lots of big ideas. Some of them come to fruition, some of them don't. She wanted to live in SoHo, so we did, but—I always felt like the asshole there. The interloper, the money guy. I didn't fit in with her friends. They were always talking about art and the artist's life. When she told me she'd fallen for one of her artist friends, I wasn't surprised. I was the wrong guy for her. I'd always been the wrong guy for her. My grandfather was right about that."

"No."

I'm startled by the anger in her voice and on her face.

"He wasn't right. He was an asshole. Things didn't work out between you and Kali because sometimes things don't work out. But you didn't miss the signs. For all anyone knew, you could have been the perfect opposites-attract couple."

"'Opposites attract' isn't a thing," I say bluntly.

Something tightens in her expression, and I instantly regret my harshness. But it's true. Kali taught me that.

She shivers. We've been standing with our shoulders out of the water, and I don't let myself look to see if she's pebbled with gooseflesh, if her nipples are hard in the cooling evening air. Not my right.

"You're cold," I say. "We should get out."

We climb out of the pool side by side, wrapping ourselves in our towels. We don't look at each other. But I couldn't be any more conscious of her.

And as we walk back to the lodge, still side by side, I can't help feeling like I've made two mistakes tonight.

Kissing her.

And stopping.

22

NATALIE

So much happened today. It's all jumping around in my head as I stand under the shower in my hotel room. All the successes, all the praise. The people I met, the things I saw. Preston with Eloise, Preston rushing off to help his sister, Preston propped over me with purple Jell-O dripping out of his hair, laughing and triumphant.

Preston's eyes, dark with heat, his mouth lowering to mine. The slick press of his skin against mine, the bunch and flex of all that hot, hard muscle, his hand on my breast, his fingers on my nipple.

The cold air on my heated skin when he pulled away.

He's right. Him and me, it's a terrible idea. Because it's like I said. I swore I'd never be the fun-times girl again.

And I don't think I ever liked Lloyd as much as I know I could like Preston.

What would it feel like to know you were just the plaything of someone you liked to the depths of your soul?

Absolutely terrible.

And *even so*, I wanted him to kiss me again.

My body is still overheated. Still bloomed and throbbing. My nipples are tight and hypersensitive as I shuck my bathing suit and stand under the hot water of the shower. When I turn to face the nozzle, the streams falling on my breasts feel like a drumbeat in my core. When I slide my fingers between my legs, I'm slick and open and swollen.

From kissing.

Kissing Preston is the best sex I've ever had. And I'm having some trouble accepting that I might not ever get to do it again.

The shower doesn't calm me down. My skin feels like it's on fire. My nipples ache. My pussy throbs. There's a constant rush of eager blood under my skin. I get out and dry myself off, still thrumming with longing. When I drop my T-shirt over my head, the brush of fabric over my breasts makes me gasp.

I slide under the covers and try to think about something else, but every road leads back to Preston. The images and sensations come, fierce and inevitable—the way the kiss started out as an exploration and became something else, something aggressive and bossy, the two of us perfectly matched in strength of will. The worshipful way his hand moved over my skin—not avoiding the softest parts of me but stopping to savor them. And the certainty with which he seemed to know how to tease and flick and caress, like he was inside my head stoking a fire he could feel, too.

In my mind, he doesn't stop. He keeps going. His hands sculpt both my breasts. His head dips so his mouth can take over from one hand, freeing it up to explore the slope of my belly.

My hand echoes that path. Enjoying the silk and give of my flesh, the softness of my curls, the plumpness of my lips, the slick damp between them. I circle my clit, pretending it's him—wishing it were him. His fingers. His tongue.

I reach for Mack, the glittery purple vibrator that's almost the exact twin—except for color—of the one Rachel handed me. I click the button to turn him on.

Ohhhh.

I clench my legs together around the hum of sensation.

It's so good.

But it's still not enough.

"All right, Big Bob," I say. "Your turn, dude."

I set Mack back on the nightstand

Big Bob, my massage wand, is not subtle. He's louder than the loudest electric toothbrush.

Can Preston hear that through the wall?

He wouldn't know what it was, would he?

Except I straight out told him I owned a vibrator.

So maybe he will know.

Maybe I hope he does.

It doesn't take long. Bob is powerful. I press him between my legs, and in my mind's eye, Preston braces himself on strong arms over me and thrusts up into me. He's big and he fills and stretches me, and I thrust back, the two of us moving in rhythm, eyes locked.

I come, muffling my cries with the extra pillow.

It's the last, and best, activity of today.

Next door, the shower turns on.

23

PRESTON—A FEW MINUTES EARLIER

Next door, the shower stops and everything falls silent. She's probably gotten into bed.

Does she sleep in pajamas? Repurposed casual clothes?

Nothing?

Does she lie on her stomach, her back, or her side?

Is she under the covers?

Where are her hands?

No.

I won't. I won't picture her.

And then I hear it. Barely. Only because I'm straining.

The thin, high-pitched hum of a vibrator.

I mean, it could be something else. Some kind of exotic white-noise machine. Her electric toothbrush.

If I hadn't heard it earlier this week, buzzing against Natalie's fingers. If the exact pitch weren't written on my brain.

Oh, *God*.

It's like an electrical charge. It races through my nerve

endings and floods my bloodstream, and my cock swells. Like she's one end of an electrode and the other is pulsing through my body.

I need my earbuds.

I dig in my suitcase, but they're not in there. Nor are they in any drawer I search. They're not on my nightstand or the desk, and it doesn't look like they've fallen behind anything. Where the hell are they?

And then, suddenly, the sound next door changes. It's not a high, tight hum, it's a deep purr.

I know that sound. It's so precise, it's like a signature. It's the Hitachi Magic Wand, one of those back massagers that doubles as—what do they call them? Intimacy aids. It has a big fat round head you can tuck between your legs, and the vibrations are strong. My ex-wife used to say it was the best orgasm on Earth for lazy people. Twenty seconds and you're done. A minute on a bad day.

But maybe Natalie's using it as a back massager.

And then I hear her moan.

Even if she's using it as a back massager, I can't listen. I'm so hard it hurts. My body is crying out for relief I don't want to give it.

I'm desperate now, pawing through my stuff for where I might have missed my earbuds, until I remember:

I last saw them on Friday. I set them down with my stuff when I was talking to Hanna in her office. And...I left them there.

I could turn on the TV. Or some music on my computer. But in order to drown her out, I'd have to turn the volume way up, and she'd hear.

She'd know. She'd know I was trying to drown her out.

I could get into the shower. I wouldn't be able to hear her in there.

I definitely can't sit here, listening for the buzz of her vibrator or the barely audible pitch of her moans, which my body tunes to like its favorite radio station. I'll go nuts.

I head for the bathroom and start the shower. Cold.

Maybe I can blame the heat of the hot springs for the loss of control. It steamed my brain. It muddled my thinking.

I step under the cold water and wait for sanity to return.

But I'm still thinking about her. About her moan when she opened to me. About the silk of her tongue against mine, the eager way she kissed. Kali *never* kissed me like that, like she couldn't get enough, like I was nourishment she couldn't live without. Not even in the beginning, and *definitely* not at the end.

And then there was the feel of Natalie's body against mine.

She's as strong and as soft as she looks. The flare of her waist and the sweet roundness of her tits feel as good as my unruly fantasies told me they would.

I want to bury myself in her.

The cold water isn't helping. Not in the slightest. It's only making me horny *and* miserable, my tight muscles starting to lock up again. With a groan, I yank the temp control into the red zone and groan again with relief when the hot water surges over me.

I reach for the conditioner and pour some into my palm. It's the hotel's conditioner, which means it's what her hair smelled like when I kissed her in the hot springs. It floods my senses, tropical and florid.

I fist my cock, pretending it's her hand wrapped around me.

Her fingers would be smaller. Softer. Smoother. More uncertain.

She'd dip her head to lick away the pre-cum that's already beading at my tip. Swirl her tongue around.

Drop to her knees. Take me into her mouth.

That tongue, the one that was so eager and needy as we kissed, it would be equally greedy and impatient as she worked my cock. She'd tease the sensitive spot where my thumb currently pauses. She'd lick up around the head, over the softest, smoothest skin. She'd suck hard there—

I lean against the shower wall, head back, struggling to keep the steady rhythm my body's demanding. My cock swells and jerks under her imagined touch, until need surges up from my balls, flaring through my spine and gut, spilling out of me, coating my hand and abs.

That's it, I think with relief. She's out of my system. From now on, I can keep my distance and focus on getting this job done.

But a few minutes later, when I've finished my shower and dried off, when I cover my head with my pillow to make sure I don't hear the slightest sound coming from her room—I know.

Biggest lie ever.

24

NATALIE

I sleep well.

Thanks, Big Bob.

And Preston.

The next morning, we meet in the conference room to debrief.

I beat him there by about thirty seconds, but it's enough that when he walks in, he draws up, startled—before he hides his surprise.

"Thank you for being prompt." His voice is a morning-rough baritone. Between the gruffness and the formality, something tightens in my low belly.

We're going to pretend nothing happened. Not in the hot tub. Not on either side of the wall afterward.

I hate it, and I like it.

Also, I like the suit. It's linen again, and so help me, I want to rub myself all over it.

All over him.

We sit down a healthy distance from each other—the hot spring having established that anything less is unsafe.

"What's next?" he says.

For a split second, my mind goes somewhere else, and then I realize he's talking about The Plan. Our Plan.

"Let's map out what we have."

Keeping our safe distance, we do it. He prints a blank week schedule, and we copy onto it everything we've come up with so far. It's more than I thought, and it's satisfying to see.

Some of the vendors have already reached out to suggest additional offerings, so we add those in. And I've thought of a few new things—there's a pottery painting shop in Bend that also does Wine and Paint nights.

"And we could do Bingo and darts," I say.

"You made fun of Bingo," he says, eyebrows raised, the corner of his mouth turned up.

I kind of wish he wouldn't do that. It reads differently now. Like a tease. Like an invitation. Which I know it isn't.

Unless it is.

"I needed to give you a hard time," I say.

The smile deepens, the dimple showing.

Gah.

I try again to convince him about axe throwing.

"No," he says. "Find something else."

"We can make it safe."

"No," he says, expression so stern it dissolves something in my nether regions.

I cross my arms. "Okay, smarty pants, then what? We need"—I count—"at least ten more programs that are compact enough to test at a summer festival but ongoing and popular enough to flesh this out." I point to the calendar.

"You're in charge of bringing the fun," he says. "I'm the spreadsheets guy, remember?"

"You can do this. Come on—it'll be good for you. Let's brainstorm. Throw some stuff out. You liked the Jell-O wrestling."

He rolls his eyes, scowling. "I didn't."

"It's not so hard," I coax. "When you need a break from work, what do you do?"

His mouth opens. Closes. Opens and closes again, before his jaw hardens, enough to tell me what I should have already guessed, a moment before he says it: "I work out."

"That's tragic, Preston."

He scowls. "It's what I need to do."

To best my grandfather, he doesn't say, but now I know that's how the sentence ends.

The things Preston's grandfather said to him, about how it would end badly with his ex-wife and about how he'd never succeed in New York—those things hadn't been only gauntlets thrown down.

They'd hurt Preston deeply. His grandfather's lack of support and faith.

He's wrapped his whole life around that hurt and refused himself anything good until he proves his grandfather wrong, like that will undo the words and the hurt, too.

I hope he's right. I hope it will. Because I don't like the idea of Preston hurting, not at all. I hate it so much, it clenches my stomach.

I think of him laughing in the Jell-O pit, before he wasn't laughing anymore. He's wrong. He *can* have fun. He just needs to let himself.

"I have an idea," I say. "I'm calling it Operation Fun."

He looks startled and slightly...terrified. Which is further proof that he needs help desperately.

"Basically, we'll figure out how to make you have fun again."

He raises an eyebrow. "Good luck with that," he says dryly.

"Did you just make a self-deprecating joke?" I ask, feigning astonishment.

"I do make jokes. Just like I do sometimes apologize."

But he doesn't sound pissed. He sounds wry and, again, self-deprecating. And it's...charming.

"Okay, so here's what I'm thinking." Ideas flood my brain as I look at him, immaculately dressed, buttoned up, a softball pitch to the part of me that lives to make other people have a good time. "We figure out what *would* be fun for you, with a little trial and error. We can throw out ideas—"

"We've already established that when it comes to ideas about what's fun, I'm stunted."

"Not *stunted*. Just...out of practice."

The corners of his mouth turn up, and there I go again, melting. For a guy who kissed me just for fun and then told me that was all it could be.

Come on, Natalie. Focus. "We try a bunch of things out, and in the process, maybe we get your mind opened up for brainstorming and help ourselves out with the planning process."

"Okaaaay..." He still looks apprehensive, but he nods.

"What are you doing tomorrow?"

"Tomorrow?" he squawks, which makes me laugh.

"Yes, *tomorrow*," I say. "As *When Harry Met Sally* says, 'When you find something that might be fun for you, you want the fun to start right away.'"

"I don't think that's a real quote."

"It applies, though, don't you think? And also, aren't you the one snapping your fingers to try to hurry up this whole operation?"

"True," he concedes. "I was going to do some work tomorr—"

"Uh-uh-uh," I caution, waving a finger at him.

"I'm free," he amends. Those unruly mouth corners are doing their thing again.

Then he frowns, his brows drawing together, and looks down at his watch. "I need to get going."

He closes his laptop and stands.

"I'll text you the deets for tomorrow," I say.

He rolls his eyes—I think at the word "deets"—then raises a finger. "Two rules."

I raise my eyebrows. "Rules? Okay."

"One. I'm paying."

I open my mouth to protest, but he glares, and I stop.

"Fair," I say. "Since I'm pretty sure your net worth is many powers of ten higher than mine, and this is your fun."

"And two..." He's walking backward toward the door as he speaks. He reaches it, puts a hand on the frame, and rakes his gaze over me from head to toe. Every cell in my body shifts subtly to point itself in his direction.

"No more kissing."

He vanishes out the door.

25

NATALIE

"Where are we going?" Preston demands as we step out of the elevator together the next day and head for the exit.

All I told him was that he should meet me in the hallway outside our rooms and that he should wear "comfy clothes." When he frowned at that, I said, *Oh, Jesus, Preston. Just...not a linen suit. You could wear what you wore to the party.*

And so he is. Running shoes, his cutoff sweats, and a soft-looking gray T-shirt that hugs every glorious inch of his shoulders, biceps, and pecs in a way that makes me wish I'd steeled myself harder against the first glimpse of him.

"I can't tell you where we're going until we get to the car," I say.

He raises his eyebrows. "You're afraid that if you tell me I won't go."

"Well, yeah."

"I keep my word," he says, scowling. "I said I'd go." He

sighs. "I know I need to do this. My lack of fun is even a liability at work right now. My boss told me 'you get it done, but you don't make friends doing it.' She said I should go out for drinks or sit around the office eating takeout."

"This situation is way worse than I thought if you think eating takeout at the office constitutes having fun. This definitely requires an intervention."

He rolls his eyes at me. "And you're the woman for the job."

"I'm absolutely the woman for the job."

"Plus," he says, "the company I'm trying to acquire for my client has in its mission statement the words *dedicated to the pursuit of fun*."

"And they picked you to work on that acquisition," I tease. "As one would."

"It just turned out that way," he admits.

We've reached my car, which he eyes suspiciously. "We should take mine."

Okay, I can't blame him for thinking that. My car is an eighteen-year-old Honda Fit inaptly named Blaze. His rental is probably a Lamborghini or something.

But we're taking my car on this outing because...

Well, because despite what he says, when he finds out where we're going, he might be tempted to flee, and I want him completely under my control.

Sort of the way he'd be if I was on my knees with his cock in my mouth, his hip bones under my thumbs.

I did *not* just think that.

It's going to be a long afternoon.

As soon as we pull away from the curb, he says, "Tell me where we're going."

I accelerate a little so he won't be able to fling open the door and roll to the curb.

"I'm not going to make a run for it," he says dryly.

"You might."

"You're scaring me."

I swallow. "Let me give you some context."

"Context is good," he rumbles.

"Since 'fun' isn't a thing in your current life, I thought we should probably tap your inner kid. You know, try to get you back in the head space you were in the last time you really had fun."

"We're going to run around the woods yelling our heads off and stabbing each other with sticks?"

"Not quite, but..." I wind my way onto the highway. "It's a trick I learned when I was doing activities planning for the nursing home. If you can get people thinking like kids, they *act* younger. I thought that might work for you."

"You're saying I'm a crusty old man."

He crosses his arms, and I can feel him glaring at me from the passenger seat, but I know him well enough by now to tell he's not really upset. "In disposition only," I say. "I've seen you shirtless."

That shuts both of us up. I'm remembering him in the hot springs, and he's—well, I don't know what he's thinking. Possibly that he regrets that kiss more with every passing hour.

"We're going to Bouncy Town," I say finally to end the silence and rid my brain of images of water droplets on a six-pack I will never get to lick.

"Bouncy—what?"

I swear he puts his hand on the door handle. Reflexively, I hit the lock button on my own door handle.

"Natalie," he says sternly. "You know what that sounds like? You and I are going to...Bouncy Town?"

I snort. "Preston Hott. Did you make a *sex* joke?"

"Absolutely not." His voice is dry and deadpan. "And if you think you heard one, you have a dirty mind."

That makes me laugh, and when I sneak a look at him, he's definitely smiling.

Maybe it wasn't a coincidence that his shower turned on right when my vibrator turned off.

"Well," I say, mock-primly, "I don't know where *your* mind is, but Bouncy Town is a party venue with trampolines and a foam pit and a climbing wall—and a bunch of other stuff. I figured we'd find *something* there that will activate your fun engine."

"My—*fun engine?*" Both his eyebrows go up, and I *think* he's not quite smirking.

It's a pretty good look on him.

"Not like *that*," I say.

"Suuuuure."

"Just...keep an open mind."

"Bouncy Town..." he mutters, but he doesn't make a run for it, and I figure that's probably good enough for now.

26

PRESTON

We start with bouncy basketball.

"Bouncy basketball?" I demand when she tells me that's where we're headed.

"It'll make sense when you see it." She leads me through the maze of small alleyways that wind between meshed-off "fun" areas. To my right, small children bounce on trampolines with reckless abandon. To my left, they throw themselves off a ledge into what I assume must be a foam pit, given that I don't hear ambulance sirens.

We arrive at the bouncy basketball space, a meshed-off area with a trampoline floor and a hoop at either end. Natalie lifts an orange rubber playground ball with basketball-like stripes from a net pocket hanging on the mesh "wall."

"They don't issue helmets for this?" I ask. "Feels like a concussion waiting to happen."

She raises her eyebrows at me. "Really? You look at this and that's what you see?"

"What do you see?"

She shakes her head and throws the ball at my chest.

I quickly discover that the physics of tramp basketball are like nothing else I've ever experienced. The ball doesn't necessarily bounce straight back up, depending on where you dribble it, and it goes instantly dead if it hits the walls.

It's a lot more chaotic than I was expecting, and my long-disused pickup basketball skills are even less helpful than I'd hoped.

But that's okay because Natalie clearly knows nothing about basketball. She runs with the ball—not even trying to dribble—and she doesn't seem to have any qualms about wrestling it out of my grasp.

In a few minutes, she's up by three baskets, and it's clear that if I'm going to have any chance of winning, I'll have to play as dirty as she is.

So I do. I twist the ball out of her hands and bounce back down the court.

"Foul!" she cries.

"Oh, *now* you want to call fouls!"

"I call 'em like I see 'em!"

She pursues me to the hoop and, as I go up, makes a sloppy grab for the ball, which bounces away from both of us.

"And that's *not* a foul?" I demand. "You can't *hug* the shooter."

"I wasn't hugging you! That was all ball."

We chase the ball and wrestle for it. She lets go suddenly, and I fall backward onto the soft surface. She tumbles down, too, landing on top of me. The ball scoots away, leaving us laughing and gasping for breath, her face inches from mine. I stare up into her dark eyes, and her smile slips.

Her cheeks are pink, her eyes sparkling. There are a few adorable freckles sprinkled across the bridge of her nose. I can feel her breath—short and quick—against my lips.

Heat sizzles in the air between us, and I become aware of the full length of her, sprawled on me. She pushes up onto her arms, which brings our lower bodies closer together. Her thighs are glorious, soft and cushiony over a core of strength, and blood surges into my groin. A minute more and I'll be hard as a rock against her.

She rolls off me before that can happen, and I regret it instantly, the loss of the warmth, the end of that moment of possibility.

"Ha!" she says, retrieving the ball.

I slowly find my way to my feet, scolding my still-heavy cock that it needs to STFU, as Natalie bounces on the tramp surface a few times directly in front of me. Nice and slow. Not too high. Just enough to put her pretty tits and her grab-able ass in motion.

That's not helping.

Her gaze follows the trajectory of mine.

"Eyes up, Hott," she teases.

"I wasn't—"

She's grinning at me. "Okay, dude," she says. "If you say so." And she makes a fake and a jab and cuts past me with the basketball, racing down the "court" and sinking her shot.

"Try to keep up, Hott," she taunts.

I scowl at her...but it's hard.

My smile keeps wanting to break through.

After bouncy basketball, we do some straight-up trampolining, which will soon be forbidden by the Geneva Conventions as a form of torture because the whole time, I'm trying not to watch Natalie's gorgeous natural jiggle.

She knows it, too. She gives a shimmy of her shoulders, treats me to a few sexy dance moves and hip swivels that make me more light-headed than I want to admit.

Fine. Two can play.

I can't dance. But I did play football in high school, and the coach believed that every football player should learn some tumbling, so we had an optional workout with the gymnastics coach on Saturday mornings. Plus, you know, we did all those box jumps. So I can get quite a bit of air—and do several different flips.

Without warning her, I demonstrate my skills.

When I finish running through my repertoire of flips and twists, she stares at me wide-eyed.

"What?" I ask, shrugging. "No biggie." And I do a few more, for good measure.

She claps and laughs, delighted.

"Preston!" she cries. "You're amazing!"

There are smile lines at the bridge of her nose and the corners of her eyes and a dimple in the sweet curve of her cheek. I feel like I've won Olympic gold, like her delight is the biggest and best prize of all. It's a rush of pure pleasure that floods my chest and wraps around the base of my spine. I want to reach out to her—

You did that once. And then realized it wasn't fair to her. Remember?

"I need water," I say abruptly.

Her smile fades, like a light going out.

We find a water fountain near the edge of the laser tag arena. A big party of kids is playing there, and we watch while we drink. Or Natalie watches them. I watch Natalie. The play of smiles and laughs across her face, the way she bounces on her toes when she's excited about something.

When did I start to crave her joy?

How can I stop?

What if I don't want to stop?

She nudges my arm. "Do you think we could have laser tag at Hott Springs Eternal?"

"I don't see why not."

"Preston," she says, eyes dramatically huge, "did you say something supportive and positive instead of telling me how expensive and dangerous an activity is?"

"Damn," I say. "You're right. I take it back."

Her cheeks are flushed, her eyes bright. I want to put my hands in her hair and pull her face to mine.

Maybe making sex jokes about Bouncy Town wasn't so far off.

"I could use a snack," I say instead of doing something I'll almost definitely regret.

We wander to the cafeteria, which is packed with kids on summer vacation. I look at my watch. Almost three forty-five. Suddenly the day doesn't feel long enough. But I don't say that; I cross my arms and tell Natalie, "There's nothing healthy on this menu."

"That's right," she says cheerfully. "Suck it up, Hott."

I like it when she calls me that. Also, I like the sound of the word *suck* in her mouth. There are a lot of things I would like in her mouth. In fact, I think there is very little about her mouth that I wouldn't like.

Jesus, Hott, pull yourself together.

It's looking less and less likely.

She orders a corn dog and a fruit salad, so I do, too. It's delicious. Or maybe I'm just really hungry.

The kids in the cafeteria travel in packs, and I quickly realize the packs are mostly birthday parties.

"There's gonna be a lot of leftover cake," Natalie says, surveying the territory. "We should get ourselves some."

"How do you propose to do that?"

She ponders, then points to a cake across the cafeteria from us. Chocolate.

"That one," she says. "Follow me."

She's about eight feet away when she looks back and sees me, unmoving. "Preston," she says. "Do you want cake, or not?"

"What are you going to do?"

"I'm going to ask if I can have a slice of cake."

"You're going to ask total strangers if you can have a slice of cake."

She shrugs. "Sure. Why not? That cake is *huge.* They've barely made a dent in it. They *need* us to help them with it."

"They're not going to let us eat their cake."

"Wanna bet?"

"Sure," I say.

"Okay," she says. "If I'm right, you have to generate a brainstorm list of fifty possible activities to flesh out our schedule. If you're right, I'll do it."

"Works for me."

I follow her over to the party.

"Hey," Natalie says. "Who's the birthday kid?"

A wild-haired, freckled eight- or nine-year-old raises his hand.

"Happy birthday!" she tells him.

"Thanks."

"Are you having a good time?"

"Yes!" all the kids cry together.

"I used to always want a birthday party at one of these places," Natalie said. "You're super lucky! And that cake looks *ah-may-zing*. Did you get it at Karl's in Bend?"

"No, Rush Creek Bakery," a woman says.

Natalie gives her an open-mouthed look. "Wait a second. You're telling me that's Nan's famous better-than-chocolate cake? That cake is sooooo good."

"Do you want some?" the woman asks.

"I'd love some," Natalie says.

And just like that, we're holding two slices of chocolate cake, walking back to our table.

"Good luck brainstorming that list," Natalie taunts around a huge mouthful of the best chocolate cake on Earth.

I can't disagree with her assessment.

"Is chocolate cake your favorite dessert?" I ask.

"As a rule, definitely," she says, her nose crinkled as she thinks about it. "My all-time favorite though...there's this bakery in New Haven, Connecticut, that I visited one time when I visited my sister at college. Lucibello's. And she ordered me this pastry—it's called a Sicilian cannoli. It's puff pastry filled with custard, and holy *crap*—I swear to God, it was *life changing*. But did you know you can't get Italian pastry around here for love or money? Maybe in San

Francisco, but it's really hard to come by on the West Coast, generally. I've had a lot of Scandinavian pastry, but the custard's not the same. I have food fantasies about Lucibello's custard all the time."

She's all riled up, talking a mile a minute, face flushed. I reach out and swipe a tiny bit of chocolate frosting off the corner of her mouth. I want to lick it off my finger so bad that I can already taste it. I lift my hand to do it, and her eyes go dark. I feel like I'm balanced on a narrow ledge, and I don't hate the rush of adrenaline it gives me.

My phone buzzes, and at the last minute, I drop my hand and wipe my finger on my napkin.

Natalie bites her lip.

I pull out my phone. It's my boss, Anjali. *Just checking in to make sure everything's going okay there. We on track with everything?*

I close my eyes and text back, *Absolutely.*

When I glance back at Natalie, she's eating cake with all her attention.

"Your birthday parties must have been a trip when you were a kid," I say.

She shrugs. "Not so much. My parents weren't big on birthday parties."

"What does that mean?" I ask. "Like, you didn't have them?"

She shrugs. "My parents were both pretty busy, and they had ideas about what was important. Chocolate cake and Bouncy Town didn't figure in. When I was nine, I started planning my own parties. That's part of how I got good at activities planning."

My chest is tight. I can imagine little-kid Natalie, a

bundle of fun energy looking for any outlet. What kind of parents wouldn't want to do everything in their power to make that kid smile and laugh?

I want to give little-kid Natalie every birthday party she never had.

"Forget that," she says, waving a hand, grinning. "Old news. C'mon. Let's go play in the arcade till we aren't so full and can bounce again."

We play Skee-Ball. I score 50,000. She scores 7,500.

"You hustled me," she accuses.

"You didn't ask if I was the Skee-Ball champion of the Western world," I point out.

"It feels like information you should have shared when we discussed whether there's anything you do for fun."

"I haven't played since I was a teenager," I say.

"And yet you're still this good."

I cross my arms. "It's like riding a bicycle."

She shakes her head, rolling her eyes. "Do you want to jump into the foam pit?"

I frown. "I don't know. I have issues with the foam pit."

"What kind of issues?"

"Trust issues. What if there are sharks?"

She crosses her arms over her chest. "You're more seriously wounded than I thought." She grabs me by the hand and drags me over to the foam pit. "We're going to jump in together."

We do. Then she goes back and does it again, this time with a flip.

"Cheer squad. What?" she asks, squinting at the expression on my face.

"Nothing," I say.

I'd been picturing her in a flippy little skirt, but I don't say that. I have the feeling again, of balancing on a narrow ledge. To vanquish it, I run and do a flip into the foam pit. It feels great, like flying.

When I come out, I'm grinning.

"Are you having *fun*?"

"If I say yes, what happens?"

She shrugs. "Probably nothing. I guess there's an infinitesimal chance the earth might stop spinning on its axis."

I give her a tiny, playful shove. She shoves me back. I pretend to stagger. Then I right myself. The expression on her face is oddly intense. She's waiting for my answer.

"Yeah," I say. "I'm having fun."

She pumps her fist. "Yes! We found your fun!"

"I guess we did," I say, and her smile gets even bigger.

She might be wrong, though. It might not be that Bouncy Town is my fun. It might be that Natalie is my fun.

She's grinning and bouncing on the springy surface under us. Her cheeks are still that pretty flushed pink, and I can't stop staring at her mouth. I take a step forward. I'm not thinking. I'm just *doing*.

But before I can do whatever it is, a form darts between us, knocking us apart. I grab Natalie's arms with both of mine to steady her, and a whole stream of children run between us like they're tucking under a bridge we've deliberately made for them.

When they've finally passed, Natalie tugs away. I hadn't realized I was still holding on to her.

"We should probably head home," she says, not looking at me. "They close soon, and the parking lot will be a zoo."

I want to take her chin in my hand, to turn her face so she has to meet my eyes. But I don't. The moment of recklessness has passed, and I remember all the reasons kissing Natalie is a terrible idea.

"Yeah," I say instead.

27

NATALIE

We're both quiet on the car ride home. I don't know what Preston's thinking about, but I'm thinking about that weird moment when I thought maybe he was going to...

Kiss me again.

It wasn't the first time today the idea had crossed my mind. There was the moment during bouncy basketball when I landed on top of him. My body went molten hot the instant his cock swelled against my thigh. All my attention narrowed onto that contact and the blooming heat between my legs. I was ten seconds from repositioning myself to have him exactly where I needed him and then lowering my mouth to his. Luckily I came to my senses and rolled off.

The temptation followed me all day, as I watched him effortlessly bowl Skee-Ball—all coiled energy and shockingly precise aim, as his heated gaze tracked the fork into my mouth, as I watched him flip and twist on the trampoline, his big muscular body surprisingly lithe and graceful.

It followed me right up to the kiss-that-didn't-happen next to the foam pit, and now it's in the car with us, and I clutch the steering wheel firmly to keep myself from—

I don't even know what I'd do. Touch his thigh, maybe. To see if he'd huff out a startled breath or a small gruff noise. To see if he'd stop me if I slid my hand higher and higher and higher, seeking what I already know I'd find, because the one thing I *don't* doubt is that he wants me, too.

Instead, I remind myself that getting kissed by him didn't turn out that well for me last time, and I struggle to think of something to say that will break the tension in the car.

But he gets there first.

"Now what?" he asks, and for a split second I think he's asking what we're supposed to do with all our pent-up chemistry. But then he clarifies, "I found my fun—now what?"

I swallow, my mouth dry. "You use that knowledge to fuel your fifty-things brainstorming list."

He nods at that.

I'm not disappointed. I'm not.

Kissing Preston won't work out for you.

I know it's true. But I'm starting to hate that it is.

WHEN WE GET BACK to Hott Springs Eternal and the lodge, Preston follows me into the elevator. I've never thought of these elevators as particularly small—but this one feels tiny now. He's just such a big guy, and I can smell all the clean parts of his scent—shampoo and soap and deodorant—

and the darker, muskier parts, too, from a day of effort. Equally, if not more, delicious. It makes me breathless, how close he feels. I struggle not to let him see it, the hard pull of air into my lungs, the rise and fall of my chest.

"So what were your favorite parts of Bouncy Town?" I ask to distract myself from the way he shrinks the elevator.

He gives it serious thought. I'm expecting him to say it was bouncy basketball or the trampoline or the foam pit because those were the moments when he came to life, but he says, "When you got us the cake."

"Why that?" I ask before I can stop myself.

He hesitates, and the pause feels heavy. Freighted. Like whatever he's about to say next will change...everything.

Instead, the elevator door opens, and I see my mom standing outside my hotel room door, leaning against the wall. I can tell she's come straight from work, gold hoops through her ear lobes, long graying hair in a bun, a stiffness in her posture left over from saving lives and making split-second decisions.

"Oh, shit," I mutter, under my breath.

"What?" he asks.

"That's my mom."

"And that's...a bad thing?"

"Long story," I say. "It's a complicated thing."

We step out of the elevator together, and my mom's eyes take in both of us, sweaty and disheveled from our day of bouncing—no sex joke there. My mother wouldn't laugh, even if there were. "Hello, Natalie," she says, her voice cool, the way it almost always is.

"Hi, Mom. Mom, this is Preston Hott, my colleague. Preston, this is my mom, Anthea Archer."

He holds out his hand to shake, and she takes it. I imagine their clasp is the world gold-medal winner for firm, confident handshakes because neither Preston nor my mom would accept anything less.

"So you're one of the brothers with the...unusual will."

For my mom, that's pretty mild, and I'm sure she considered and discarded quite a few other words before she chose that one, like *absurd* and *legally indefensible* and *outrageous*.

"That's me," Preston says. "Natalie and I are working together on meeting the terms of the will, and also on building a great program for Hott Springs Eternal."

My mother's expensively groomed eyebrows arch. "So I hear. Natalie's lucky to have your help. Not many activities planners get to benefit from the insight and expertise of a New York investment banker."

Preston's face doesn't change. His voice doesn't, either. When he speaks again, it's polite—friendly, even—and level. He says, "Oh, but it's exactly the opposite of that, Mrs. Archer. I'm lucky to have hers. There's no way I'd be able to make any of this happen without her. What Natalie does is way harder than she makes it look and far more valuable than rearranging the wealth of the top one percent. Bringing lots of people joy isn't something everyone can do. And there aren't many people who would do it with as much grace and good humor, not to mention imagination, as she does. I'm very much the lowly assistant in this scenario." And then he turns to me. "Thank you so much for all your help today, Natalie. I can't tell you how grateful I am that you're so open to helping my family with our situation."

He turns back to my mom. "I don't want to intrude on your time with your daughter," he says. "I'll leave you two to your chat. But it was lovely to meet you."

And then, without giving my mom a moment to respond, he unlocks his room and disappears into it.

28

PRESTON

"**H**ey," someone says behind me.

I'm neck deep in the hot springs, the night velvet dark around me, and the voice is Natalie's.

"Mind if I come in?" she asks.

"No."

I don't want to stare at her, but it's impossible to look away as she sheds her robe, treating me to a full-length view of her in that goddamned bikini. She's perfect: smooth, curvy, generous. I want to lick every bare inch, then remove the small cloth triangles that hide the rest of her and lick there, too.

Maybe my eyes say what I'm thinking because some-thing hot flickers behind her gaze before her eyes shutter and she slides down into the water beside me. Not too close. A safe distance away. But close enough that my chest tightens and my cock thickens and want turns from a vague, abstract thing to a deep tug on my spine.

"I looked for you earlier..." she says.

"I went out for food."

I was mad enough to spit nails when I closed the door behind me after my introduction to Natalie's mother. Natalie didn't deserve the way her mom had casually torn her down. No one does, but especially not Natalie, not after what she'd done for me. For my family.

For what felt like the twentieth time, I needed to get the hell out of my room, or I would burst through the wall like the Incredible Hulk, this time all rage. So I went for a run, showered, grabbed dinner, and came down here for a soak.

Natalie shifts, sending ripples through the water that tease my over-alert nerve endings. "I wanted to thank you," she says quietly. "For standing up for me."

"You don't have to thank me." It comes out gruffer than I intend.

"Well, it was—really nice." She bites her lip, shyly. "No one has ever done that for me."

"Then they're fools." The words spill out before I can help myself. "Like I was at first."

That makes her smile. "I converted you, huh?"

"Maybe."

Her smile gets bigger, and I lose my words. I trail my fingertips along the surface of the water and don't let myself stare at her the way I desperately want to.

"Your mom—" I begin.

She makes a sharp noise.

"What did she say to you? In your room?"

"You heard us?"

"Not the words. Only that you were talking."

Natalie raises her eyebrows, but we both choose to skate

over the implication: that her walls are thin enough for plenty of sounds to carry.

"She wanted to let me know that a doctor I worked for a few years back is willing to write me a letter of recommendation if I apply to schools."

"Schools?"

"Nursing administration, a bunch of other possibilities. It's part of my Get Serious About a Career plan."

I'm unable to imagine Natalie behind a desk, doing soul-numbing paperwork, all the wild joy bound up in her blood and bones instead of out there in the world. "Why would you want to do nursing administration?"

"There are a bunch of other things, too, not only that—they're medical field jobs with great ratios for how much it costs to get the degree versus how much you can make, and they all have good earning and advancement potential—what?"

I'm staring at her.

She bites her lip.

"Is that what you want?"

"I..." She rubs her thumb over her bottom lip, drawing my eye there, and I have to make myself look away rather than lean in to bite the plump flesh. "I've had it on my to-do list for months to look at the brochures and websites. And I...never do. I don't think—no, I *know*—I don't want to." She takes a deep breath. "I *love* my job. I wish my mom could see that. She wants me to do something with long-term prospects. A"—she crooks her fingers in quotes—"career."

I make a sharp sound of frustration. "She's not being fair to you."

It sounds blunter and more presumptuous than I mean

it to, and I want to take it back. Especially in light of how unfair *I* was to Natalie in the beginning.

She looks away. "She and my dad are high powered. She's chief of surgery, and my dad's a retired state supreme court justice. My sister's a biochemical engineer, and her hubby is some corporate hotshot doing global whatever it is. I'm not like them. And I've always been the kid who— underachieved."

"Who they perceived as underachieving," I correct.

Her eyes flick to mine, and there's something bright and hopeful in them. I think of her saying that no one had ever stood up for her before—and what kind of bullshit is that?

She closes her eyes, opens them again. "When I was in high school, I came downstairs one night and overheard them talking about me. My mom was asking my dad, 'What *does* having fun all the time equip you for?' and my dad said 'Not much' and laughed."

"Jesus," I breathe, rage rising in me again.

"Then my mom said, 'It's like she was born completely without ambition,' and my dad said, 'She's the one we'll have in our basement till she's fifty.'"

She reports it coolly, unemotionally, and a band cinches around my chest. "Natalie."

She waves it off. "Whatever. I know they never meant for me to overhear it. They were worried about me and blowing off steam."

"They shouldn't have said it," I say roughly. "Because it was cruel, but also because it's not true. You're—" I have to stop because the words feel so big they're half choking me. "You're good at what you do, and what you do matters.

You're funny and generous and giving and *fun*. So fuck them if they can't see that."

"Preston."

Her voice breaks on my name, and it scoops out my chest. All the logic and caution, all the excuses and reasons go up in flame, and I turn my body toward her, finally doing what I've wanted to do all day, taking her head in my cupped hands and lowering my face to hers.

Her mouth is soft, and she opens to me right away, without hesitation. She lets out a small gasp, and it undoes me. I clutch the back of her head, swallowing her moans, running my tongue along her lip and biting it to make her moan again.

The kiss is on fire, my cock already so hard I can't help but tug her toward me, and she comes readily, willingly, *eagerly*, pressing her slick belly to me, giving me pressure and friction. I want more of her, though: I want to fit us together, all our opposites perfectly made for each other.

Without breaking the kiss, I lift her up and set her on the side of the pool, and she scoots herself forward, spreading her thighs so I can step between them and notch my hardness to her soft heat. Steam rises off her skin; the air is cooler than the water.

"Preston," she moans.

"Is this okay? Is this what you want?"

"Yes, *please*," she whimpers.

"Can I touch you?"

"You'd better."

I reach for the strings of her top, and my hand ghosts over her skin, raising goose bumps and drawing a whimper from her. I untie both bows and let the top fall. She makes a startled sound as the air finds her nipples, and I watch, cock hardening in sympathy, as they tighten against that cool brush. She watches me watch her, and there's something raw and hungry in her face.

"Like this?" I ask.

It's the lightest touch. The pads of my fingers skimming the peak barely harder than the air brushed over her. But her nipple tightens more.

"It makes me hard, watching your nipples get stiff," I tell her.

Her mouth opens. "Preston Hott, are you talking dirty to me?"

I can't hold back my smile. "I guess I am."

I stroke both nipples as lightly as I can, watching the play of pleasure across her face. Then I dip my head and take one into my mouth. It's a tight bead against my tongue, and I flick the tip, loving the taste of her skin and the moans I draw out of her. She pushes closer to me, trying to get more contact between my cock and her pussy, and I cup her ass and yank her closer because I want it, too. Fuck, I want it. Now she's tipping her hips and rubbing herself against my erection, and it's not only the sensation—which is fierce—but also knowing that she's chasing her orgasm that makes me feel like I'm going to lose it. I pull back, and she groans.

"Tease."

"It's too good, you going for it like that. Taking what you need. It's too hot."

"Preston."

"Hold still and let me give it to you. Don't chase it."

"God," she moans. "You're going to kill me."

I dip my head again, teasing, swirling, biting, working those hard nubs—one, then the other—until she dips a hand between her thighs and grinds herself against it. I tug her hand away and twist it behind her back, and she says, "You're so *mean*."

"Trust me," I say. "Just trust me."

Her other hand tries to take its place, so I pin both behind her while I return to tonguing her nipples, until she's rocking her hips against empty air.

"Preston, please," she begs.

"What do you need?"

"I need to come."

"How do you want to come, baby?" I ask, the endearment slipping out. I've never used it before, but there's something about this moment that's different. Some rawness and tenderness I don't even know how to name.

"I want to come on your cock," she pleads, and I want that, too, so fucking bad. I picture it: taking my cock out, yanking her bathing suit to the side, easing into her. The fact that we're in a semi-public place, that we don't have condoms—those things don't matter in this wild, taut moment.

But I also don't want this to be over, exploring her, teasing her, making her wish for things she can't have yet from me. I want to surprise her and make her wonder and want.

I guess I want to be her fun for a while.

So I step close again, give her my cock through my board shorts and her bathing suit, and she takes what I'm offering with a groan of gratitude that almost makes me lose it. I wrestle myself under control again and play with her nipples, and she rubs against the hard, swollen bulge in my shorts. It only takes her maybe ten rocks of her hips before she's coming, crying out, cursing triumphantly— and this is what almost takes me over the edge with her— telling me *you're so good, so fucking hot, Preston, just like that, you did this, this is all for you.*

29

NATALIE

What surprises me most is the way he holds me afterward. Both arms around me, one hand cupped behind my head, tucking it to his chest. He says *shhhh* and rocks me. It's so unexpectedly tender and I'm so wrecked by pleasure already that my eyes fill up with tears.

We stay like that for a long time. He doesn't ask for anything back. He's still hard between my legs, and I can feel his cock jerking from the contact of my body against his, but he doesn't push or press or seem to have any needs at all outside of wanting to make me feel cared for.

Who *is* this version of him?

And how can I keep myself from falling for him?

Because, shit, I think I am.

But the facts of our situation—they're still basically the same. He has to go back to New York, and I want to be here in Rush Creek, doing the job I finally admitted to myself I want indefinitely.

That's even assuming he wants more. And there's no reason to think he does.

Well. Maybe this:

You're good at what you do, and what you do matters. You're funny and generous and giving and fun. *So fuck them if they can't see that.*

But that's not a promise. It just means he likes me. Not that he wants to *be with* me.

I draw back, needing to put space between us. He goes unwillingly, letting go of my head, unwrapping his arms. His eyes track over my face like he's trying to read my thoughts. I feel exposed, certain he'll be able to tell I have feelings I shouldn't have.

He doesn't say anything, though, only reaches for my bikini top and helps me put it back on, urging me to turn around so he can retie it. Even that bit of tenderness makes my eyes tear again...and *what is wrong with me?*

I guess I just haven't been with guys who believe in aftercare.

Restored, I slide back into the hot water, crossing my arms over my chest like that's going to hold the feelings inside.

Fat chance.

We're both silent, and that makes me nervous. One of us should say something, make light of the situation or at least acknowledge what happened, maybe make an observation about what should come next. I could offer to reciprocate, which wouldn't be a hardship at all. I'd love to wrap my fist around his cock. I'd love to make Preston Hott lose control, watch him fall apart.

But as I'm wracking my brain for the word or the gesture to get us there, we both hear a sound behind us. Someone's rattling the gate. There are voices, a man's and a woman's, laughing, and I hope we're not about to get an eyeful. I check to make sure we're decent—we are—and Preston's doing the same, eyes roaming over my swimsuit and then down to his own.

The gate swings open, and Sonya and Quinn step in.

"Well, hey," Sonya says, grinning at us.

"Oh, hey," Preston says, and I can see the dismay on his face. He didn't want to get caught like this by his brother and sister-in-law. It does look pretty incriminating. Hostile coworkers usually don't soak together late at night.

"We, um, interrupting anything?" Quinn uses the same dry tone that Preston is a master at.

My cheeks go lava hot.

"No," Preston says succinctly—which, for what it's worth, is true. "I was in here, and Natalie came by to take a dip. She offered to leave, but I said it was no big deal and she could stay."

Okay, so that's our story and we're sticking to it. Part of me is glad he protected my dignity—not the best look to be getting off on the boss's brother's cock in the family-owned spa—but the other part of me is bummed that we're his dirty little secret.

"I was about to get out," I say.

"Me, too." Preston delivers those words, then swings himself up and out of the pool; I have to not swallow my tongue at the sight of those muscles, long and ripped and lean, hard at work in arms that look like they were made for my personal enjoyment. His body is even more tempting now that I've had it between my thighs and can attest to how perfectly it fits there.

"Don't feel like you have to leave. We can come back another time," Sonya says, lips curved in a smile she can't hide. "Or we can all hang out."

I shake my head. "We're good." I follow Preston up out of the tub. "But it would be fun to all hang out sometime. I'd be up for that."

Preston gives me a look. Right, I probably made things worse, implying that it makes sense for the four of us to hang out, like on a double date. Or maybe I'm overthinking it.

We make our excuses, grab our stuff, and say our good-byes. I follow him out and back toward the lodge. When we get there, we ride the elevator in near silence.

I think it'll be awkward when we get to our rooms, but as we approach my door, Preston crowds me against it and puts one hand up on the frame over my head. *Oh.*

I've said it out loud, and he grins.

His big body brushes mine. *Ohhh.*

He ducks and kisses me, and it's not a quick goodbye kiss, either. My body roars back to life, and I'm ready to drag him into my room—when his phone buzzes.

"Sorry, I gotta—" He looks at it. "Shit," he says. "I have to deal with this before the Asian markets close."

"No worries," I say, trying to sound nonchalant.

"I might be up a while," he says. "See you tomorrow? In the office?"

"Sure. See you tomorrow."

And I go into my room first so I don't have to watch him retreat.

Once inside, I give myself a stern silent lecture.

I tell myself that it makes absolutely no sense to feel shitty about the fact that a workaholic who lives on the other side of the country preempted making out with me to *be a workaholic who lives on the other side of the country.*

30

NATALIE

Unsurprisingly, I sleep like shit.

I alternate between replaying the events in the spa and the moment outside my door, between fantasizing about touching Preston and telling myself to chill the fuck out and not get attached.

I get to work exhausted and looking it, which makes me feel even more vulnerable. I brace myself for the possibility that Preston running away last night was the end of the story.

So I'm not surprised at all when he stalks into the meeting room, sits down across from me without making eye contact, and gets straight down to business.

"I did the fifty-things brainstorming list last night," he says briskly.

Was it before or after you did that thing with your tongue, where you flicked and circled my nipple?

Before or after I said, Preston Hott, are you talking dirty to me? *And you smiled and said,* I guess I am.

Preston Hott, it turns out, is *fun*.

There are lots of fun men in the world. A million of them. A billion, maybe. But this one?

He didn't know he was fun, and that makes it so, so much better.

Because he's fun just for me.

Heat flares all over my body, remembering.

Except now he's not. Now he's all buttoned-up business again.

"I couldn't sleep—"

My eyes flick to his face, but he's said it without any particular emphasis or significance, and he's not looking at me.

"—and I kept thinking about Bouncy Town—"

Then he does look at me, for a split second, and I think maybe he's going to acknowledge the dirty joke, acknowledge what happened...

But he turns away again and goes on: "—and I came up with a lot of good stuff, but my best idea is: I think we should add Nerf blaster tag. I kept thinking about the kids playing laser tag—but Nerf is less expensive. And less messy and less painful than paintball."

Trust Preston to still be thinking about practical considerations. It makes me smile a little. "I don't know," I say slowly. "Both laser tag and paintball track when you make a hit. Nerf blasters would have to work on the honor system."

"I thought of that," he says. "We'd have to test if it would work. We could get some of the Hotts and Wilders together again and run a test this weekend. I was thinking we could use flags, like in football, but you'd have three of them, and each time you get hit you pull one, so people can see how many chances you have left." He lifts his chin. "I was also thinking—the will doesn't say we can only run each activity in one slot. We could have Nerf tag every night at seven thirty. There are a lot of other things we could run two or three times in a week. We wouldn't have to come up with that many more ideas, and we could get to work right away on prepping for the festival."

"Ooh," I say. "That could work. I like it."

The corners of his mouth tug up, and he casts me a pleased sideways glance that's almost shy. This big, competent, powerful guy who wants to get the answer right on the quiz. I want to throw my arms around him.

I want to push him down on the table.

I sigh and do neither.

We spend the rest of the meeting divvying up tasks, placing rush orders for materials online, and talking about the logistics for the festival itself—volunteers, setup and cleanup, and spreading the word. The festival has its own marketing, but we'll need to advertise our booth through social media to make sure we get enough participants to make the activities fun.

We have to get those five stars.

By the time we're done, I'm caught up in the excitement, and I've almost—but not completely—forgotten how confused I am about the gap between what I want and what I can have from Preston.

"Well," Preston says. "Thank you. That was extremely productive."

"Yeah," I say. "Good work."

"You, too." He doesn't look at me, just stands and gathers his things. It's like we've reset back a week and a half, lost all the progress we made. It's like we never opened up to each other, played with each other, touched each other.

It's like he never made me fall apart in his arms and then held me, and my chest aches, reminding me that I'm in deeper than I want to be.

But that's my own fault, for sure. It's not like there was ever a reason to believe Preston would be interested in more than a little fun with me.

I'm staring down at the table, so I hear rather than see the door open. Then close again.

I heave a sigh.

Then I hear another, more unexpected, sound—a *snick*. I look up and find that Preston's still on this side of the door, locking it. His eyes meet mine and hold.

Hang on. What...?

Now he's drawing all the blinds on the meeting room windows, still watching me. His gaze hungry, predatory.

My spine goes hot and liquid.

He stalks toward me. Turns me in my swivel chair. Plants both hands on the table, on either side of me. Lowers his mouth to mine.

The sound I let out—small, broken—is equal parts raw lust and relief. He makes a matching sound, a rough, dark grunt, and kisses me deeper, like he's trying to swallow me. Then he's kneeling at my feet, drawing me to the edge of the chair.

"Very convenient choice of clothes," he growls, gripping

my calves. Sliding his hands up, up, over my thighs, under my loose skirt. I never wear skirts, but something made me put this one on this morning, some tiny hopeful single brain cell that pictured this very thing. He buries his face against the thin fabric of my lacy panties and breathes. Nips, the perfect small bite of pain on my tender flesh.

I moan, and he reaches a hand up to cover my mouth. "Shhh," he says, hot air teasing through the lace, against my clit. "You have to be very, very quiet, or I'll stop."

"Don't stop. Please," I whisper, raking my teeth against his palm and drawing a hiss out of him.

"Not a sound, then."

I obediently press my lips together under the seal of his big, warm hand, and he goes back to work between my legs. Sliding my panties aside, licking his finger before pressing it to my already swollen clit. And *ohhh*. He knows what he's doing, starting light, watching my face closely until he gets the reaction he wants and then dialing in, right there, perfect pressure, testing all the possibilities: a featherlight up-and-down stroke; an almost-painful flick; a soft, spiraling circle, until he gets that just right, too, and I whimper, so turned on my hips are rocking in the chair.

He stops. "I said not a sound."

I clamp my lips together.

"Are you going to be a good girl?"

I nod wildly.

He licks his finger again, and I throw my head back against the seat and arch my back, sounds fighting their way up my throat, but I won't, I won't, because oh, God, I don't want him to stop—not what he's doing now, perfect circles, perfect size, perfect pressure, and then, like that's not enough, he takes the hand off my mouth so he can ease two fingers into my core, thick, curled, skillful, and I'm arching, shattering, mouth open in a silent scream, coming in thick glorious spasms against his touch, around his fingers.

31

PRESTON

Natalie coming on my fingers is my new favorite thing *ever*.

I would like it to happen at least once per day, preferably several.

She eases herself into an upright position—having thrown herself back into the seat—and smiles at me. She's wrecked—pink-cheeked, red-mouthed, glaze-eyed—and beautiful. I'd like to keep her like this all the time.

But she has other ideas.

"Switch places," she says. She slowly stands, her legs still shaky—which I fucking love. "Sit."

I raise my eyebrows at her.

"Preston," she says. "Sit the fuck down."

But I don't, because I love the heat in her eyes right now, the spark in them, and I want to see what happens if I don't. Instead, I suck my fingers, savoring her, and watch her pupils flare hot and appreciative.

"Fine, then," she says and shrugs. Her mouth lifts into a

wicked smile, and she drops to her knees in front of me. Cups the bulge of my erection through my suit slacks.

"What do you think you're doing?"

"Sucking you," she says, the words so perfectly, deliciously dirty that my cock jerks against the constraint of my boxer briefs and trousers.

"Jesus, Nat," I rasp out.

She works my belt free.

My cock is thick, flush. Getting her off made me desperate with lust. And watching her hands on my buckle and my button and zipper?

I didn't know I could be this hard.

And apparently I can still get harder because now she's tugging my briefs down and tonguing the head of my cock.

Hot as fuck.

"Natalie," I groan.

She stops, and I groan again.

"Hush," she says, waggling a finger up at me. She's beautiful on her knees like this, looking up at me through long lashes, cheeks still flushed from her own pleasure, naughty intentions written all over her face. "Not a sound from you."

She's delighted to be giving me a taste of my own medicine; I bite back my smile.

Her tongue's on me again, circling, finding the wetness at my tip and savoring it, licking long caresses down my shaft, then coming back up to work the sensitive spot under the head. I almost say her name again but stop myself, sliding a hand into her hair instead. Not to control her depth or speed, just to be touching her. I want to touch her all over. If her mouth didn't feel so fucking good on my cock, I'd force her to her feet so I could kiss and touch every inch of her. I'd lay her out on the conference table and settle my mouth between her legs.

Instead, I watch her lips wrap around my cock and try with every ounce of my waning self-control not to thrust into the wet heat of her mouth as she sucks and licks and takes me deeper than I'd ever ask for. I never assume anyone's throat is for my taking, but Natalie's giving and giving in a way that I can feel to the root of my shaft and deep in my balls, and the pleasure is rich and thick, gathering like a storm. I tug her hair, trying to warn her without sound, but if anything, she's licking harder, sucking me deeper, humming a little at the back of her throat like she loves the feel of me there.

"Natalie—" I break my silence to warn her. "I'm close—"

I think she'll pull off. That she'll say, *Shh*, that she'll tell me to be quiet, but that's not what happens. She doubles down, and the hot swirl of her tongue, the feel of her swallowing me, gathers heat at the base of my spine, need surging up.

"I'm going to—"

Her hand comes around the back of my thigh, locks there, tight, and it's that—the bossiness of it, the sureness of it, the explicit invitation—that pushes me over the edge, and I'm coming hard down her throat, and she's swallowing, the contractions of her throat mingling with the spasms of my cock, her hums and my soft helpless groans tangling in the quiet air of the conference room, until we're both quiet and still.

She pulls off slowly and looks up at me.

There's no other word for the expression on her face but *smug*.

"That was—"

I discover I can't even finish the sentence, which only makes her smirk deeper.

"I've never had a work blow job," I say instead. Pretty sure I lost about a thousand brain cells a minute ago.

"Maybe you have the wrong job?" she suggests, grinning and wiping her chin.

There's a knock at the door, and we frantically reassemble ourselves, both our fingers overlapping in a desperate effort to get my fly closed and my slacks buttoned.

"Pres, you in there?" Hanna asks from outside.

We're laughing so hard it's making it even harder to fumble our way back to mostly presentable. Natalie scans me, and I do the same back, and we both give nods of approval before I hurry to the door and unlock it.

"Was that locked?" Hanna asks.

"I don't think so," I say. "Maybe jammed or something?"

"Did you pull the blinds?" she asks, looking around.

"Nah," I say. "They were like that. Someone must have pulled them this morning. Maybe the sun was at an awkward angle."

"Huh," she says. "Anyway. I had a couple of questions for you…"

Over her head, Natalie gives me a wicked, wicked grin, right before she slides past me and disappears out the door.

32

NATALIE

"Gotcha!" someone cries, before something tags me behind my right shoulder blade, a sharp but not unpleasant pinch.

It's Lucy, one of Hanna's many sisters-in-law, lowering her Nerf blaster and aiming a significant glance at the two flags hanging from my waistband. I pull the second-to-last flag and aim back at her, firing—but I miss. She dashes back into the woods.

Preston's test run for the Nerf tag idea is absurdly successful. He sent an email to all the Hotts and all the Wilders asking if anyone could help us out by mocking up a small Nerf tag game. We were hoping to get at least six players, probably mostly kids.

Instead, the response was overwhelming. Five Wilder brothers, their wives and girlfriends, their sister Amanda and her husband, everyone's kids, Quinn and his wife Sonya, Shane and his fiancée Ivy, all of Sonya's coworkers, Ivy's sister and her girlfriend—even the Wilder siblings' mom Barb and her wife Geneva (who, yelling battle cries, silver hair flying, turned out to be the most badass competitor of all) played. Lucy's mom, also a grand dame, played distance-tagger from an upstairs window of Hanna's house, because her Achilles was hurting her and she didn't think running was a good idea.

She tagged Preston down to one flag about ten minutes ago.

A flash of blue behind some nearby trees draws my attention.

It's Preston.

"I see you," I call, loading, taking aim, unleashing. Missing.

I haven't landed a tag yet. Darts are apparently not my strong suit.

A dart flies from behind the trees, narrowly missing me. I'm in the open and he's in the shadow of the woods. I'm a sitting duck. I make a run for it across a patch of grass, throwing myself into a small grove of bushes. Another dart whizzes by as I take cover.

And as I do? I see the flag. The big prize. The one I'm supposed to bring back to headquarters for my team.

I reach for it.

A dart comes from a totally unexpected direction and pings off my upper arm.

"Damn!"

Preston's laughter comes from the same direction as the dart. He joins me, lifting the victory flag from where it's dangling from a shrub. He pumps his fist victoriously, grinning ear to ear, one blue flag still hanging from his belt. His joy is little-boyish, contagious. It makes me absurdly happy. This is the same guy who dryly wished me luck when I told him we'd figure out how he could have fun again.

"Hey," I say.

"Hey," he says back.

"Your game is a big success."

He grins like I've told him he won the Nobel Prize in Economics. "I was nervous," he admits. "That it wouldn't work. That it wouldn't be fun. I'm new to this."

The admission, and the blushing pride in his success, is so freaking cute. Preston Hott is *adorable*. I think of the guy I met my first day, the one who refastened his cuff links so my undignified behavior wouldn't rub off on him. Or— that's what I'd thought then. Maybe no one had given him permission to have fun in so long, he'd forgotten that he could.

"Preston," I say. "That first day. When you walked in on me dancing—"

"Oh, God," he says, rubbing his forehead. "You broke my brain, Natalie. I was so tightly wound, and you were—"

I don't know how he's going to finish that sentence. *Too much*? *So over the top*?

"So fucking hot. And then you grabbed my tie and—I had to get out of there before you saw how hard you made me."

My mouth falls open.

His curves up in a wry smile.

"I thought you hated me."

"I know," he says. "And maybe for a second, I thought I did—you reminded me of all the things I'd told myself I couldn't have. I was determined not to want anyone who was different from me again. I'd basically decided to only have one-night stands until I met some woman who took her professional life extremely seriously and would be contented to overlap for a few hours in bed a couple times a week."

"That sounds like hell," I say frankly.

"Yeah," he says. "It doesn't sound great to me now, when I say it out loud." He takes my hand and swings it between us. "We should get back so I can officially claim victory. See how everyone's fared. See if they have any feedback for us."

He has to sneak back, to avoid being hit, but he makes it to Hanna's porch and pins the flag to the small target he set up earlier for that purpose.

"Victory!" he cries, and players drift back to the house, clutching their blasters.

When everyone's done congratulating him (and roasting Gabe Wilder, who leads hunting trips as part of his job, for not managing to tag a single player), we do a debrief.

Everyone loved it. They gather around Preston, raving about what a good time they had. He's got that pleased-as-punch expression on his face again, the one that makes me feel like I've won something—instead of getting my ass whupped.

"Don't thank me," he tells his assembled fans. "Thank Natalie, who got me out of my 1980s team-building mentality. She's the genius behind most of the new programming —which you'll get to experience at the festival next Saturday. You'll all be there, right? And tell everyone you know."

And shit.

I've been so busy feeling victorious, so busy being thrilled for Preston and me that we're on our way to success that I let myself forget what this is all about. Why we're doing this. The festival *is next weekend*. We're almost done, we've almost made it, we're *killing* it, and our grand prize is:

This is over. I get my job, Preston goes back to New York and gets his promotion.

Everyone gets what they want.

I should feel ecstatic...but I don't.

33

PRESTON

"So," Shane says a few minutes later, "have you learned your lesson yet? Whatever point Granddad was trying to make? Because I'm still not sure I know what mine was."

The three of us—me, Shane, and Quinn—are lounging against a tree not far from Hanna's house. Natalie's on the other side of the yard, helping Hanna's sister-in-law Amanda set out food.

Shane doesn't even look like he broke a sweat during the Nerf proceedings. Since he moved back to Rush Creek, he's been embracing the cowboy-chic thing and wearing untucked button-downs, jeans, and cowboy boots. Today he's even got an expensive-looking cowboy hat tipped at a slight angle on his too-good-looking head. Maybe movie stars don't sweat.

"Your lesson from Granddad was *Don't be an asshole*," Quinn grumbles. "And mine was *I should have let you eat the poisonous mushroom.*"

Shane snorts. "You're never going to let that go, are you."

Quinn scowls. "It was a big missed opportunity to get away with murder." But he gives Shane a fond shove with his shoulder.

"I've learned a few lessons," I say, shrugging. "Like Shane shoulda let me invest his earnings from the first *Crown of Spires* movie because if he had, he'd be as rich as I am now."

Shane rolls his eyes. "So you got lucky a few times."

"I got *smart* a few times," I say.

He shrugs. "I mean, after a point, rich is rich, right?"

Quinn clears his throat, and we both turn to glare at him. "Yeah, yeah, we know," I tell him.

"I'm just saying." He lifts a shoulder. "There's rich, and then there's *rich*."

Quinn makes Shane and me look like paupers by comparison. Also, in contrast to his wealth and to our movie-star brother, Quinn exists almost exclusively in well-worn nerd T-shirts. Today's says, *I try to tell chemistry jokes. But there's no reaction.*

"So," Shane says. "Speaking of Granddad and his fucked-up lessons, what do you think he's got cooked up for Rhys and Tucker?"

Sonya and Ivy join us, Sonya laying her head on Quinn's shoulder. Her forehead crinkles. "I mean, it would be pretty awesome if the guy whose job is literally breaking up marriages had to get married."

"Ooh," Ivy says. Her girl-next-door prettiness gives Sonya's elegant polish a run for its money. "Are we talking about Rhys? I've been thinking about what your granddad is going to do to torture him."

"Yeah," Sonya says. "I'm betting on some kind of arranged-marriage thing."

"But would your grandfather actually *do* that? Even with Shane and me, he didn't *make* Shane get engaged to me. It just sort of...happened." Ivy cocks her head. "It's not clear whether he even knew I existed. I'm almost like a side effect."

Shane grumbles, "You make it sound like we tripped and fell into a fake engagement."

"It was a little like that." Ivy shrugs. She snuggles up to Shane's side and rests her head against his shoulder. "In the best possible way." She smiles up at him, and I watch Shane's expression go gooey. "Maybe Rhys will trip and fall into a fake engagement, too."

"With who?" Sonya asks.

Shane snorts. "Clearly someone who has elaborate dreams of lacy white weddings with all the trimmings. Rhys *hates* weddings."

"Are we talking about what Granddad is going to do to Rhys?" Hanna asks, bumping up between Shane and me. "Because I'm totally convinced it's going to have something to do with wedding planning. Can you see it?"

We all nod. Because we really, really can.

"Oh, hey, and this is weird. Did you know one of my clients knows him? Apparently he represented her husband in their divorce. She didn't know Rhys was my brother when she booked at Hott Springs Eternal. She spotted him in a family photo and was like, 'Wait a sec.'"

"Ha, that's hilarious!" Ivy says. "So Rhys got her

divorced, and you're getting her married again. You're like her angel and her devil. Is it awkward for her, though? If she runs into Rhys?"

"Gonna try to keep that from happening," Hanna says. "He's not around much. Shouldn't be too hard."

"Famous last words," Shane mutters. "Everything always proceeds according to plan around here."

We're all quiet for a moment, contemplating that. I sneak a look at Natalie; she's laughing with Amanda, head thrown back, curls bouncing, and something in my chest tightens and warms.

"And Tucker? What's Granddad going to do to Tuck?" Quinn asks.

We all look around the circle at each other. Lately Tucker's been even grimmer and more absent than usual. He lives in Rush Creek now, but recently he hasn't joined the fray much, not unless we pressure him to. We've been trying to leave him alone, let him work through...whatever it is.

"It would be like kicking a puppy," Sonya says softly, and there's a murmur of agreement around the circle. "Maybe he won't get an assignment."

"And maybe monkeys will fly out of my butt?" Shane offers. He turns to look at me. "I'm going to address the elephant in the room here. What's going on with you and Natalie? And don't say *Nothing*. The two of you looked awfully chummy coming out of the woods together."

"And you've been spending a ton of time in that conference room together," Hanna supplies. "With the blinds drawn."

Five pairs of suspicious eyes pin me.

Traitor. I glare at her. She shrugs as if to say, *Just telling it like it is.*

"Nothing," I say.

The suspicious expressions get, if anything, more suspicious.

"Come on," Shane says. "Quinn and Sonya, Ivy and me...you and Nat? That would make a perfect track record for Granddad's shenanigans. Three happily-ever-afters."

My throat tightens.

"Don't," Quinn says. "You'll scare the boy. He's at a vulnerable moment right now." He smirks at me. "You have to walk through the fire before you can embrace the happily-ever-after."

"Quit it," I say grumpily. "Grandfather isn't some kind of magic ghostly matchmaker. Not everyone is going to end up with happily-ever-afters. Not all of us even want them. Some of us might have thought we had them and realized they're bullshit. Maybe my happily-ever-after is getting this shit done, getting my ass out of here, and getting back to New York City so I can get my deal signed."

I become aware of a disturbance in the circle of friends and family around me. Big eyes and coughs and Hanna's not-terribly-subtle hand across the throat in the universal signal for *Cut!*

"Hey, everyone," Natalie says smoothly, joining the circle, smiling around at us.

34

NATALIE

"He's just freaked out," Sonya says, behind me.

I turn, overstuffed plate in hand, to find her holding a similarly packed-to-the-gills selection of Amanda's international appetizers.

"Preston," she clarifies. "Quinn was the same way at first. The Hott brothers take a while to—settle down."

"It's not like that," I say. "It's just—we're just—"

My shoulders slump.

She puts a hand on my arm. "Welcome to the club," she says. "Women whose lives have been turned upside down by Fox Hott, usually known as 'Granddad' or 'my fucking grandfather.'"

I smile.

"Did you know him?"

"A little," she says. "I liked him. He was a curmudgeon, but his heart was mostly in the right place. Not that you can tell from the amount of chaos he's wreaked after death. Although I think even Quinn and Shane might grudgingly concede that he's done more good than harm. So far." She shrugs. "You may beg to differ."

I shake my head. "No. I wouldn't undo meeting Preston and getting to be"—I hesitate, smile wryly—"friends? With him."

"Honey, I don't think friends look at you the way that man looks at you. Like he hasn't eaten for a month and you're a make-your-own-sundae extravaganza."

"You caught him at a bad angle," I say. "He was probably ogling the food table."

She smiles. "Okay," she says. "If you say so. And whatever is or isn't true of you and Preston, I'm glad you're working at Hott Springs Eternal and I'm glad we're getting to know you. And I hope you'll keep hanging out with Ivy and Reggie and me."

"I'd love to," I say.

She smiles at me. "Good. Now. Tell me what you need Reggie to do next weekend at the festival, nail-wise."

"Natalie!"

Preston must have followed me from Hanna's place to the lodge and caught the elevator behind mine. He jogs down the hall now, lean and athletic and fully at ease in that gorgeous body of his, his face lined with concern.

"Natalie. I'm sorry. I—"

"No," I say, cutting him off, waving a hand. "I get it. And you were right. It's not a *happily ever after* kind of thing. There was never any expectation that it might be. You weren't saying anything I wouldn't have said, too, if they'd put me on the spot like that."

He opens his mouth, but I'm on a roll, eager to get the words out before he can do something awful, like apologize for leading me on.

"This, us"—I gesture between us—"it's you getting a chance to finally do what you want to do, just *because*. On impulse. And I don't expect more from you than that. I certainly don't expect happily ever after."

He's shaking his head. Hard. "No," he says. "What I said was harsh. Rude. And I didn't mean it. My brothers get me riled up, and—look, Natalie, whatever happens next, what's happened between us so far is..." His gaze holds mine, warm and earnest.

Hope rolls through me, with a sweet kick of adrenaline. "*Real.*"

He reaches out and takes both my hands, wrapping them up so they disappear in the size and strength of his. "It's real, and it was special to me. It wasn't following an impulse or scratching an itch. I did what I did—kissed you, touched you—because I like you. A lot. Because I wanted to be closer to you."

God. His words. That's a lot of truth from a guy who a couple of weeks ago would barely talk to me. All of me softens, all of me yearns toward him like a flower toward the sun—but I hold myself back because even if all that's true...

He's leaving.

I can't let myself forget it.

"Thank you," I say quietly. "Me, too. I felt those things and wanted those things, too. But maybe we should—" I sigh, because there's such a gulf between what I want and what I should want. It's so hard to make myself be smarter this time around, but I don't want to find myself in another coffee shop watching a guy I thought loved me gaze into another woman's eyes like they hold the secrets of the universe. "Maybe we should be realistic about this situation. And, you know, call it quits before—before either of us gets hurt."

His eyes move over my face, taking me in. Warm and slow and soft. "That would be the smart thing to do, wouldn't it?" he asks.

I know what he's asking. He's asking me to tell him it's okay for us to be impulsive. To do this because it's fun, just...because.

But I can't. I can't be his just-for-fun girl.

"Yeah," I say. "And, um, I'd better—if you don't mind, I need a shower."

I turn away and wave my door key over the card pad.

THE HOTEL DOOR on its hydraulic hinges takes an interminable amount of time to swing shut behind me. I stand for a moment, waiting for the telltale snick of the thick lock. I want to be left alone so I can shower and cry and lick my wounds.

Now I know the truth I've been hiding from myself.

I don't want him to leave.

Worse, I want him not to want to leave.

The door still hasn't shut. What's taking it so long?

There's a thud behind me.

I turn.

Preston's there. Arm up over his head, palm flat on the door, bracing it open, lean muscles corded. His expression is stern, like the way he looked the first time I saw him. But he's wearing a T-shirt and a pair of shorts, and his hair is disheveled from Nerf tag.

He stalks into the room, toward me. My heart picks up, skittish prey under the hunter's gaze. Then he stops. His expression changes. Not the hunter's. Something much more uncertain. Agonized, even.

"What?" I ask.

"For fuck's sake, Natalie," he says. "I don't know what the hell I'm doing in here. And I *never* don't know what I'm doing. I just—"

His voice is rough, catching on the words.

"—know I can't stay away."

And then the door clicks shut and he's pressing me against it, kissing me even more breathless than I already am. His big body crowds mine, musky and delicious, the rigid bar of his cock pressing against my hip. A rush of desire floods my belly and core.

This. This is what I want.

Preston scoops me up and carries me into the bathroom. Setting me down, he points a finger at me. "Clothes off." His tone is bossy, and I like it. So much.

We strip in parallel, and he reaches in and starts the hot water. He climbs in first and holds the curtain back for me. When I step in, he opens his arms and draws me close. His body and the water are hot, and I'm overwhelmed by the rush of sensation. Tears prickle my eyes as I cling to him, and he hugs me right back, tight, like he knows.

He picks up the soap, lathers up a washcloth. His hands

on my body are sure and confident, and the perfect intersection of sensual pleasure and being cared for makes my tears prick even harder. I'm glad we're in the shower and it's not so obvious that being soaped clean is making me cry. His hands are gentle everywhere he touches, but I still moan when his washcloth-covered palm passes between my legs, and he laughs, a dark chuckle.

He watches as I shampoo my hair, his eyes traveling everywhere, touching my naked body as surely as his hands did. And his gaze makes goose bumps rise, makes my nipples pinch.

"My turn," he says, low and gruff, so I shampoo his hair, and he groans at the scratch of my fingernails over his scalp, rubbing back against my fingertips like a cat asking for more, more, more. I take the washcloth and soap him, and his face goes soft and vulnerable at the pleasure of being touched and tended to. I want to make him this soft —and also hard and desperate.

The soap washes down the drain. He kisses me, water pouring over both our heads, everything wet and hot, his palm traveling down my body and making me moan again, his fingers slipping into my folds. He growls when he finds me slick there, his mouth greedy against mine as he plays a moment, trailing his fingers in a tease around my clit, then a quick dip into my core that makes my knees buckle. He cranks the water off, grabs a towel, wraps me in it. He ties one around his own waist, then scoops me up and carries me to the bed, where he deposits me. He tugs me to the edge of the mattress and kneels between my thighs.

"God," he says. "You're so pretty." He extends a finger and parts my folds gently, stroking lightly over my clit. I lift my hips for more, and he laughs, that dark chuckle again, promising dirty goodness. He focuses his attention on my clit as my body turns liquid and I shift my hips restlessly.

He lowers his mouth, his tongue replacing his finger, his fingers finding my core, wet and ready for him, and he licks me, small, tight circles, while his fingers slip inside me. They're long and thick, and he plays, looking for the combination that will make me bow off the bed. When he finds it—tongue circling my clit, two fingers curled into my G-spot—he exploits it relentlessly until I'm coming, helpless, arching, crying out, trying not to pull his hair too hard.

He slowly withdraws his fingers, slides them into his mouth, savoring me, while I watch. "Condoms?" he asks.

I gesture toward the nightstand because I don't think words are my friend right now. I feel empty and needy, swollen and desperate. His eyes rake appreciatively over my body, and I return the favor because he's standing next to the bed and his cock is so hard the head is glossy and swollen, a drop of pre-cum rolling over the stretched skin.

"I want that." I point, and he gives himself a single rough stroke before rolling the condom on.

I wonder if he's going to tease, make me beg for it, but he doesn't. He eases himself over me, his thighs between mine, and kisses me. Open and ravenous. I lick into his mouth, trying to show him how wet I am, how much I need him, and he must understand because he groans and settles, that thick cock against the seam of my lips, sliding down, lining up.

"You want this?"

"Yes," I groan, and then, on the sweetest, deepest kiss, he gives me just the tip. He works me open so patiently that my core clenches around him and I think I might come again just from that. From the stretch and his care.

But I don't. I tingle and glitter and burn and *want* as he glides deeper, stretching me more, my body infinitely willing to have him, those inner muscles tightening involuntarily around him, until he's buried to the hilt. And then he starts moving, slow at first but deep. Thorough. My body is awash in wonder at the sensation of him. He watches my eyes, intent on me, and moves faster, finding a rhythm that makes me gasp and clutch at his shoulders. Then we're kissing again, the silky slide of our tongues echoing the slick friction of his cock in my core.

Maybe it's because I just came, maybe it's because the shower woke up every nerve ending in my body, maybe it's because he's so goddamned good at this, his hips hitching up over mine at the end to give me something to rub against, but I can tell I'm going to come fast and hard. I don't want this to end too soon, but I'm not in control. Not of the rhythm, not of my pleasure, not of the way it feels to have him in my bed, my arms, my mouth, my body. I ache all over with it, and the ache winds itself into a thick knot of urgency. I clutch him closer and kiss him deeper and come all over his cock, a wild, enormous, seismic shattering. He breaks the kiss and buries his face against my neck, his body going rigid, his breath whispering across my skin, hot and desperate as he pulses inside me. "Natalie," he groans. "Natalie. Natalie. Natalie. Natalie."

He keeps saying it until it's only a hoarse whisper.

35

———

PRESTON

I'm wrecked.

I lift my head slowly to find Natalie watching me with an amused expression on her face.

"That was—" I attempt. My voice sounds like sandpaper.

That makes her grin even bigger. "It was pretty good."

"Pretty good?!"

I can barely move, but I can still manufacture outrage.

"All right," she admits. "It was fucking amazing."

It's my turn to grin. Summoning all my resources, I manage to withdraw from the clutch of her arms and the heat of her core, condom safely secured, and get myself to the bathroom to toss it. I come back with a warm washcloth. I gently stroke it between her legs, and she closes her eyes and hums with pleasure. I clean us both up, then settle back into bed next to her.

We lie on our sides, facing each other. "I wish you didn't live in New York," she says.

Startled, I meet her eyes. "I wish I didn't, too."

It stays between us for a moment before she looks away, giving a short, dark laugh. "No, you don't," she says. "Not really. You definitely couldn't do finance in Rush Creek."

I want to argue with her, but we both know that at some fundamental level, she's right.

"Then I wish you lived in New York City."

She winces.

"What?" I ask.

"I mean…"

"Not a fan of New York?"

"I visited with my sister. That same trip when we ate the pastries. And—no. Not a fan."

"It's a terrible place to visit, but you might like to live there."

The corner of her mouth turns up. "Said no one, ever." She sighs, the almost smile vanishing. "I don't think you really wish I lived in New York, either. We have—very different lives."

"Yeah," I say. "I work seventy-hour weeks and never have any fun, and you—"

She laughs. "Work seventy-hour weeks that are all fun, all the time."

"You wouldn't want to leave this job."

"I wouldn't," she says. "Not now that I know it's what I really want to do."

I brush her hair off her face, stroke a hand over the soft, sweet roundness of her cheek. "Besides. We'd never see each other. And you'd hate me after a while, for putting work first."

Her eyes move over my face. "Kali did?"

"Kali did," I affirm.

She thinks about it a second. "And you'd get bored of me."

"I wouldn't," I insist.

"You say that now, but..." She frowns.

It's my turn to read her unhappy history on her face. "Lloyd did," I fill in.

"Lloyd did." She sighs. "It's okay. Some things are just meant to be—what they are. I think this is one of those things."

"I could fly out sometimes. I have a jet."

She rolls her eyes. "You have a fucking jet," she says. "See, that right there? That's why this couldn't work. I mean, what would that be? You'd be my sugar daddy and I'd be your booty call, and—"

"You deserve better?" I hazard.

Her face softens.

"You do, too," she says.

We're quiet again, taking each other in. Her hand reaches for mine between us and clutches, surprisingly tight.

"I don't do this, you know," she says.

"What?" I ask.

"Lloyd was...well, he was sort of right about me."

"Lloyd was full of shit," I say roughly.

"He was right about the fact that I don't really do... serious."

I think about what I know of her. All the people she touches, all the joy she brings.

"You're good at being the life of the party," I say because all of a sudden I can see what's been right in front of my eyes all this time. "But it's never your party. You have friends, but you don't have—"

"I don't have *people*," she says.

You have me, I want to say. I can feel the words on my tongue, their exact weight and heft and...consequence.

But she doesn't, does she? We just talked through all the perfectly rational reasons I can't stay here and she can't come to New York. And at the bottom, there's this fact: I can't put my whole life in another person's hands again.

So I say, "I'm here now"—as much for myself as for her —and then I cup her face and make her look at me until her gaze softens again. Until we fall toward each other and we're kissing again. Until I am just hands and skin and a mouth.

I lose track of everything except the idea of making her feel good.

36

NATALIE

I stretch, my body deliciously sore from Nerf tag and the multipart workout Preston subjected me to last night. We made love three times before falling asleep in the early morning, and now the clock tells me it's almost noon.

I reach an arm out and encounter—cool sheets.

I roll over and face the empty half of the bed, and even though he could be anywhere—the bathroom, next door, getting me coffee—my stomach knots.

Because it's only a matter of time until he's *gone* gone.

Then the room door opens and Preston walks in, grinning. "Hey, sleepyhead. I brought you some treats."

I haul myself to sitting, arrange the sheet around my top half as best I can, and take in the glorious sight before me:

A large, extremely handsome man in a T-shirt and jeans, holding out two white paper bags from which delicious smells are emanating.

"Rush Creek Bakery." He holds up one white bag. "And Carol's Cakes." He holds up another. "I know they're not as good as the ones from that place you went to with your sister, but I thought it would be fun to do a comparison."

"Did you say," I tease, "it would be *fun*?"

"I did. Look at me, finding the fun all by myself, right?" He heads for the hotel room desk—where I was dancing that first night when he walked in—and starts to take the pastries out of the bags. Then he looks over at me, considering. He tilts his head. "Would it be more fun to eat them in bed?"

"It *might*," I say. "But would that cause you psychic pain? Crumbs and everything?"

He looks from the bags in his hand to the pristine hotel sheets and back again. Then his gaze falls on my hand, which still clutches the sheets to my chest, and his eyes darken. "Well," he says, considering me with lingering, slow regard, "it *might*. But that might be canceled out by all the other possibilities that arise from eating pastries in bed."

I pat the bed next to me, and he kicks his shoes off and slides in beside me, dropping a kiss onto my head. "Hey," he says. "Last night was amazing. You were amazing. I've never said that to anyone before because it never felt true enough to say—but I want you to know. It wasn't just—"

He stops.

And I get it. I get why he's hesitating. I think he was going to say *It wasn't just sex*, but if it wasn't, then where does that leave us?

"It's okay," I tell him. "It was amazing for me, too. I want to do it again. Definitely. As soon as I...eat. And shower. And maybe brush my teeth and wash my face."

That makes him laugh.

"We can definitely do all those things."

He unrolls the tops of the white paper bags. "I got a chocolate croissant, an apple turnover, and a cream-cheese Danish from each, so we can subject them to careful analysis. It wouldn't—"

"—make sense to compare apple turnovers to orange-cream doughnuts?" I ask.

"Ha. Exactly."

I love that Preston's idea of fun is careful analysis of these pastries, that he's being so thorough and rigorous about it all. I love that he's probably dying to make a spreadsheet right now. I love that he listened to what I said about my favorite pastries, that he thought to bring me pastries for breakfast the morning after, that he told me how he felt about last night (because honestly, most men don't bother). I love—

But I've run out of words. There's just this...ache.

"Did you know Carol made pastries?" Preston demands.

"No!"

"I didn't, either, until Nan—you know, owner of Rush Creek Bake—"

"Everyone knows Nan."

"Right. She definitely makes an impression. Well, she said that several years ago she started making cakes because she felt like it wasn't good for Rush Creek that Carol's Cake Shop was running a monopoly—"

I'm shaking with laughter at Preston's Nan imitation— puffed up and soapbox-y and dead-on.

"So then—Nan says—after she started making cakes, Carol got vengeful."

I raise an eyebrow. "I love how when Nan does it it's social justice and when Carol does it, it's vengeance."

He grins. "It's all about point of view. So Carol started her pastry business to give Nan a run for her money."

"What's next?" I ask. "I mean, obviously Nan has to do something. She can't let Carol's awful behavior stand."

"Right. It sounds like maybe pies are next?"

I snicker. He hands me a chocolate croissant. "Is this *warm*?" I ask, wide-eyed.

"I had them heat them up. They're better that way, right?"

"So. Much. Better." If I wasn't in love with him before, I am now. I lick chocolate out of the little cleft at the end of my croissant. "Mmm," I moan, then raise my eyes to find Preston watching me.

He carefully takes the croissant out of my hands and sets it on the bag on the nightstand.

"Are you *sure*," he asks quietly, "that you need to do all those other things first?"

And then he leans in and kisses me in a way that makes the correct answer to that question obvious.

37

NATALIE

The week flies. I spend almost every waking moment working on our festival offerings, which also means getting them ready to offer at the resort. It's a lot of work and a lot of fun. Preston and I drive all over creation retrieving materials, like a big white tent and a plastic shower curtain that will jointly form a splatter room, an even bigger kiddie pool for Jell-O wrestling than we used at the party, a few additional sets of football flags, and more Nerf blasters and darts. We talk to Amanda about catering snacks for our booth next weekend, then recruit her kids and a bunch of other Wilder kids to letter signs for us. When the kids turn out to be fantastic workers, we ask them to help us out on festival day.

There are a few hairy moments, like when we realize that there's a roof leak in the corner of the stable where we've stored the Jell-O powder and have to order more, shipped overnight. Another one when the company we subcontracted horseback rides from bails out on us for a kid's birthday party in the ritziest part of Bend. But we chip away at the problems.

Meanwhile, whenever he's not needed, Preston is on work conferences. Or in something he calls a *virtual data room*, supervising *due diligence*. Or working on spreadsheets, tap-tap-tapping away on his computer. And except when we're doing heavy lifting, he's mostly wearing his fine, expensive button-downs with the sleeves rolled, exposing the loveliest typing porn this side of the Mississippi. I could watch him make spreadsheets all day, those long, blunt fingers, whose strength and agility I am well-acquainted with...those distinctly male wrists...the sinewy muscle in his forearms, that extra bulge of strength right below his elbow...

Often, Preston gets interrupted mid-spreadsheet.

I ask him a lot if things are going okay with work, the deal, and the promotion, and he assures me they are. His client, a company called MegaStar, is almost done studying the company they want to gobble up, called PowerFun and so far, everything's gone smoothly. No surprises. In fact, he might be able to stick around Rush Creek for a little longer, wrap up due diligence remotely, then go back to New York to finish negotiations.

I let myself lean into that "a little longer." The open-endedness of it. It probably shouldn't, but it gives me hope.

And then, suddenly, it's Friday night, the night before the festival. Preston is in his room, doing something complicated requiring Asian market hours, while Hanna and I close and lock the door on the Hott Springs Eternal barn stall, where all tomorrow's materials are stored. Hanna has had a lot of questions for me, which is a little weird because she's been pretty hands off with all this stuff so far. But tonight she wants to know a slew of details about how the programming will work, exactly when it will start, and so on.

It takes me a while to extricate myself, and when I do, when I head back to the lodge, I'm as weary as I can ever remember being. I want food and sleep. And I feel a little grumpy because there's nothing in my mini fridge except moldy leftovers I keep meaning to throw away, and I'm tired of all the Hott Springs Eternal room service options. I guess I'll get another Bleu Hott Burger—calories are good—but it doesn't sound appealing.

I'm so tired and hungry that I lean my head against the elevator wall while it rises and have to make myself step out and plod down the hall to my room.

I swipe my key card and jump back with a shriek, because there's someone in my room.

Then I realize it's Preston, and—

"Oh, wow," I say. "Wow. *Wow.*"

I'm frozen in the doorway, mouth open.

He's borrowed a table from somewhere else in the hotel, covered it with a tablecloth, set it with china and candles and—

"Preston—" I'm still at a loss for words. There are two platters and three big bowls of food, everything family style —chicken parm, manicotti, Bolognese, rigatoni and broccoli, something that looks like penne alla vodka. "Where is this *from*?"

He hesitates.

"Bella Italia?" I name a place in Bend.

"Carmine's," he says.

"In Bend?"

"In New York." He looks a little sheepish. "It's my favorite takeout in New York. It's my pump-up takeout. What I eat the night before a big presentation or meeting or deal."

"Holy—"

Tears fill my eyes.

"Nat—" he says helplessly.

"No, it's good crying. It's—I was so hungry and tired, and this is—better than sex."

He laughs. "Don't say that."

"Better than sex with men other than you," I correct myself, and he laughs again and kisses me.

"Sit." He sweeps my chair out.

"How did you get me takeout from New York?" I sit and spread my napkin out as he does the same across from me.

"Franklin."

I recognize the name of his assistant from work conversations I've partially overheard. "He flew it out. And Hanna kept you busy for a while."

Oh. Hence all the questions.

"You—" I'm still having trouble with full sentences.

"I've always wanted to do something like this. Ridiculous. Extravagant. Just *because*. On impulse. For fun," he says and the corners of his eyes crinkle, and the last vestiges of me, the last parts I was holding back from him, give themselves up.

"I love this," I say, because I won't say what I really mean.

He points with his fork. "Dig in."

I do and moan into the first bite.

"Nat," he warns.

We've been over this a few times this week; he really likes how much I love food. "Don't worry," I say. "I'm too hungry to do anything except eat."

"You've said that before," he says.

Pretty much before every meal this week.

But we do eat. We eat and eat, until he says, "Save a little room."

"What for?" I ask.

He opens the closet and pulls down a box. A white box with red writing on the top, tied with red-and-white string.

"That's—"

My mouth is hanging open again, my brain frozen on the sight.

"Lucibello's," he confirms.

He pulls the string free, opens the box, and shows me the contents. Flaky tube-shaped pastry, thick custard cream —I'm flooded with memories of sitting in my sister's dorm room, licking my fingers clean, and my mouth waters.

"You got me...?"

I get up, take the box out of his hands, set it aside, and smother him in a bear hug. He laughs and kisses me.

"You got me Lucibello's. Oh my God, Pres, are you trying to destroy me? What am I supposed to do when you leave? You've ruined me for other men."

"Good," he says. His eyes are dark and serious on mine. "That was my plan."

"But—"

He holds me tighter. "If I could get Carmine's and Lucibello's here, don't you think I could get myself here any time I wanted?"

It takes me a minute to understand what he's saying. Asking. "You mean—long distance?"

His gaze probes mine. "If you're willing to give it a shot."

"Yeah," I say, breathless, not giving myself time to think about it, just—wanting what he's offering. "Yeah."

"I couldn't be here all the time, but look how much I was able to do remotely, right? And no crises that called me back into the office or anything."

"And I could fly sometimes, too. You could send the private jet for me."

His eyes crinkle with laughter. "I could."

We stare at each other, and I'm so full of him, of what I feel for him that I don't know how to put it into words. I'm going to need another way to show him.

And maybe he can see because he smiles down at me. "Do you—um—" His smile gets deeper. "Want to take a little break before dessert and—mmm," he says, as I answer with my mouth on his, pulling him toward the bed.

38

PRESTON

All we do for a long time is kiss. Her mouth, soft and open and yielding, on mine. It's kissing for kissing's sake, slow and undemanding. Languid. And it sets me on fire, my whole mouth tingling, my skin buzzing with sensation, every nerve ending gathering itself into the thick, angry demand of my cock. I need her now, and I could do this forever, and I can't decide which would be better.

So I take another route. I kiss along her jaw to her ear and explore the curves of the delicate shell; I huff warm breath against her until she arches and moans, her hands grabbing my clothes. I trail down her neck and throat, then pause to take her shirt off. Her bra. I kneel over her and take her in, because she's beautiful. Perfect. Round and full, nipples tipped with a dark rose and already peaked for me. I kiss across her collarbone while she squirms under me, trying to press closer, trying to get friction on her needy clit and pussy. I don't let her, though. I make her wait, loving her whimpers and moans.

I trail kisses down the slope of her breast, teasing the tip of one nipple. Then the other. She arches toward me, offering me more, but I don't take the bait.

"You're a tease, Preston Hott," she says huskily.

"You're worth the wait, Natalie Archer," I tell her, and then I draw spirals on one breast, circling from the outside in, closing on the tight nub of her nipple. Teasing over it once, twice, again. She's worked my thigh between hers now and is rubbing against me, and I use both my hands and hips to pin her because I don't want her coming too fast. I want to take my time with her. I want to make her desperate.

"You're mean," she whines.

"You like it."

I take off my own shirt because I love the way she looks at me. The way her eyes go hazy and unfocused, the way they linger and admire. I could watch her watch me all day, and if that makes me an egotistical bastard, I'll take it. Except I'm not as patient as I think I am; as I strip off the rest of my clothes, my cock is demanding, my mouth is hungry for the feel of those nipples, my hands want her smooth skin under them. I go back to work, licking my way down her belly, lush and bitable. My teeth find the waistband of her capris, and my hands take over, pull them down, and then her panties. I settle myself between her legs, shoulders pushing her open, one hand reaching to keep up my tease, flicking the tips of her breasts, taut and beaded.

It takes all my self-control not to grind myself against the bed, but I want to give her everything I've got, so I make myself keep still while I run my tongue up her seam, opening her so I can see her sweet, swollen clit, so I can lick it, so I can make her lift her hips and grab my hair and call my name. She does, and I lick more, harder, circling her.

"Preston," she whimpers.

"What do you need, Nat?"

"I want you inside me."

I groan.

"Now, Pres."

"But I'm not done tasting you, baby."

It's her turn to groan, and she shifts her hips impatiently against my face. I slide two fingers inside her, loving the way her body clenches around them. I tug her clit between my lips, suck so gently, withdraw my fingers from her so I can hold both her hips still while I suck harder until I can feel the tension gathering tight in her.

It's tight in me, too, my cock leaking precum at the tip, hard and shiny and so full of need. It bobs against my belly as I kneel up between her legs, and she reaches for it, pupils blown, mindless and eager. I have to pull away because if she touches me, I'll come all over her, and I want to be inside her, want to take her with me and feel her all around me.

I take the condom she offers and roll it on, then press into her slowly because I want to watch her while I do it. The way her eyes shift over my face, reading my reactions. The way we're winding each other up, her pleasure, my pleasure, her need, my need, her tension, my tension. Where we're joined, I can't tell where I end and she begins or who's moving. I only know that we're finding a rhythm together and it feels like the whole world is caught in that rhythm. She pulls me down so my body is pressed against hers, the whole length of me. My cheek is flush with hers, and we move and move. It's like the kissing was earlier, fucking for the sake of fucking and not to finish, slow and silky and molten, and I decide I don't want to come at all, I want to stay like this with her for as long as she'll let me.

Except our bodies still have other ideas, and she's moving restlessly under me. She can't stop trying to rub at the end of the stroke where it rucks up over her public bone, she can't stop trying to get me deeper, she can't stop squeezing me, and even if I could stop myself from thrusting, which would be about as easy as stopping the sun from rising, she wouldn't let me, grabbing my ass and pulling me in, tight, close.

"Don't stop," she tells me urgently. "Please don't stop. I never want you to stop."

It's the *never* that gets me in the end, and I'm coming, big, long, deep pulls of pleasure, rigid over her, pressing where she needs me, until she's coming, too, still telling me she never, ever wants me to stop.

I'VE NEVER BEEN A CUDDLER. More the kind of guy who rolls back to my side of the bed and glories in the righteous power of a king-sized mattress. But Natalie makes me want to cuddle. Maybe it's the way her head fits perfectly in the crook of my shoulder or the way she throws an arm over my chest or the way she settles with a small, trusting sigh.

"We're gonna be great tomorrow," she says sleepily.

"We're already pretty great," I say.

I can feel her smiling, mouth lifting against my bare chest. Her body grows heavier and warmer as she drifts toward sleep.

But sleep doesn't come for me.

I'm awake tonight. Wide awake. And it's not because I'm worried about tomorrow. Far from it. Tomorrow will be great. People will love it. We'll rake in the five-star reviews.

And it's not because I'm not relaxed. That sex wrung every last drop of tension from my body. Sex with Natalie doesn't feel like a workout. It feels like a conversation. It feels like fun feels when you haven't had it for too long, a little bit of party and a lot of revelation.

No, I can't sleep because I can't imagine leaving and I can't imagine staying, so I'm suspended in between.

My phone shows me midnight, then 1:00 a.m., and I gently ease myself out from under Natalie. She clutches at me and makes small sleepy sounds of protest.

"I'm going to take a walk," I whisper. "Do you want to come with?"

"Are you crazy?" she murmurs back roughly, and I laugh, and she's asleep again before I can answer her.

I get dressed, take the elevator downstairs, and head out into the summer darkness. There's a half-moon tonight, and the grounds are deserted. I wander by the ranch house, then down to the river, lighting the narrow path with my phone's flashlight. I skirt the cottages and campground and head back up, past where Hanna planted a tree for our mom.

A shadow moves by the stables, and I freeze.

It moves again, a human form shifting toward the stable entrance.

What the fuck?

I take a step, meaning to surprise the intruder, but years of sitting behind a desk in New York have apparently overridden my childhood forest sense because as soon as my foot lands, a stick crackles underneath. The figure startles —then bolts.

I chase them, but they're faster than me, despite the regular exercise and running. I hear an engine start in the distance, probably at the main road, and I know I've lost them.

I call Tucker and wake him up.

"You in Rush Creek?" I ask.

"Yeah," he grunts.

I tell him the situation. "All the stuff for tomorrow's festival is stored in the stables. If someone got in, they could—they could totally mess us up."

"Did you make sure it's all okay?"

I dig my keys out, keeping him on the line, and check, but it's all there, and intact, and I heave a big sigh of relief.

"Do you think it's related to the other sabotage? What happened with Hott Spot and the flood, and what happened with Tobuary's wedding?" I ask him.

"We don't know either of those things was sabotage."

"True, but—it's a lot of coincidence. And then for someone to show up tonight...?"

"You want me to come out there and keep an eye until tomorrow morning?"

"You'd do that?"

I don't mean for there to be so much surprise in my

voice. I was there for Quinn when things went to shit. All of us were. And all of us were there for Shane when he was facing down the cancellation of the wedding that would fulfill his letter from our grandfather. Still, somehow it feels different when it's me. It feels...nice.

"'Course I would," he says offhandedly. "Hold tight. I'll be there in a few."

39

NATALIE

Festival day dawns bright but not too hot—perfect summer weather. All the Rush Creek–based Hotts and their spouses, fiancées, and friends show up to help us with setup, and it's done in a flash. Soon Preston and I are seated in our booth, waiting for the festival to officially start.

"Did I dream it, or did you go for a walk in the middle of the night last night?" I ask Preston.

"You didn't dream it."

"What?" I ask because there's a weird expression on his face.

"Nothing much," he says. "I surprised what might have been an intruder, messing around near the stables. Tuck came and kept an eye, so there's no way they could have gotten into our stuff, but—it's weird. It's not the first time something strange like that has happened."

He tells me two wild stories—one about Quinn and a flood, and one about Shane and a wedding...and I have to admit, it doesn't sound like coincidence. Three brothers, three wacky will assignments, and three incidents where they almost couldn't fulfill their obligations because something happened at the last minute.

Well, in our case, nothing happened, but only because Preston was in the right place at the right time.

"So you think it could be…sabotage?"

"I think it's possible," he says. "When the wedding disaster happened with Shane, we thought it might be Arthur Weggers, our grandfather's attorney. He's been a thorn in all of our sides. But I don't see what he'd have to gain from undermining us."

"Who does have something to gain?"

"Blue Iron Mining," Preston says grimly. "The company that gets the land if we don't comply with the will."

"Jesus. That's effed up."

"I'm going to have Tucker do a little…investigating. Oh," he says, shoulders squaring. "And speak of the devil. Not that devil. The other devil. Hi, Arthur."

"Hello, Preston," says a small bald elderly man. "Excellent job you've done with all this."

"I had a lot of help," Preston says. "Arthur, this is Natalie Archer. She'll be running the programming after I go back to New York, and she's helped me develop it."

Weggers considers that for a moment, frowning. Then he gives a slight nod. "That wasn't against the rules," he says. "Hello, Natalie."

"Nat, this is Arthur Weggers. Esquire."

Preston says this last with a mock gravitas that makes me want to giggle.

Our other staffers are arriving, so I leave Preston and Weggers to their conversation, showing all our helpers what I need them to do. We're essentially running a mini festival inside the big festival. By the time I get everyone set up, people have started arriving. Our booth is mobbed, and I give an internal fist pump of delight.

Weggers has appointed himself master of ceremonies in the meantime, a kind of circus ringleader. He calls out to people as they arrive, corralling them into lines and directing them to our various activities.

He's also put himself in charge of ethics. Everyone who participates in any activity scans a QR code and leaves a star rating. Weggers makes sure we don't hover over people as they review us. "It would be unfair for you to exert undue influence over their selection," he says sternly.

I swallow that giggle, too.

We can barely keep up with demand, and most people want to try all the activities we're offering. When I check out our ratings so far, we're operating at a solid 4.8. (There's a one-star review from someone who didn't like the hot pretzel bites because there were only four mustard options and none of them was stone ground.)

Our best customer, it turns out, is Nan of Rush Creek Bakery, who has left her shop in the care of her grandson and is participating in every last activity.

"I'm giving you five stars on everything," she tells me.

Weggers, lurking nearby, straightens and steps our way. "There's no need to disclose that," he tells her primly. "It creates the suggestion that you might have been bribed—"

"Oh, shut your flappy trap," Nan says. "Mansplainer."

This time, my giggle escapes. Weggers gives me an outraged look.

"I'm going to play Nerf tag," Nan says.

"That doesn't seem age appropriate," Weggers says primly.

"Listen, you old bag," she says. "I'm at least five years younger than you."

"But you don't see me playing Nerf tag. I'm keeping my dignity and my knees intact—"

"Because you're a dried-up coot," Nan says. "Watch me." And with a challenging look over her shoulder, she trots off in the direction of the Nerf tag stand.

"Wretched misery," Weggers mutters. Then, to my utter shock, he heads off after her. I must make a startled sound because he turns around.

"Someone has to make sure she doesn't kill herself," he says and shrugs.

"Did that happen?" Sonya asks, appearing at my side. "I didn't hallucinate it, right?"

"It definitely happened," I say.

A moment later, Nan runs past me, blasting Nerf darts over her shoulder. She's followed close behind by Arthur Weggers, cursing creatively.

Sonya and I can't stop laughing for several minutes.

40

NATALIE

Later that day, Hanna helps me unpack another truckload into the stable stall. Then I drive back to where I left Preston. In the meantime, he's finished disassembling the splatter tent. He's standing over the pieces like a hunter over a wildebeest, looking triumphant.

"You guys okay without me for this last load?" Hanna asks.

"Totally," I say. "You get back to Eloise and Easton."

She heads off in their direction, and the two of us start loading up the truck with the last of our stuff.

"You did it," I tell him. "You fulfilled the will."

"We did it," he corrects. "I couldn't have done it without you."

"So. You're free to go."

He shakes his head, his expression serious. "I don't have to leave yet," he says. "Due diligence is still in progress, and negotiations won't stop till those are done. I'm guessing I have at least another week? Maybe more?"

A week sounds like bliss to me. I lean toward him, his mouth comes down hungrily on mine, and I know we're going to celebrate today's win in the best possible way in a few minutes.

Except right then I feel the vibration of his phone against my hip. Not the single buzz of an incoming text, but the insistent rasp of a call.

"I should probably get that, huh?" he says.

I nod.

He pulls his phone out, reads the screen, and curses.

"Anjali?"

"Yeah," he says.

Anjali's his boss—and, I've learned, the only call he'll take any time of day or under any circumstances. Well, not any. I've been delighted to discover that when Preston's giving me his, shall we say, *undivided attention*, it's definitely undivided.

He answers it. "Hey."

After a moment of silence, he says, "What do you mean, an issue?"

More silence, then, "Why am I hearing this from you?"

I take a step away to give him more privacy, but he shakes his head, meeting my eyes—he doesn't need me to go.

His voice is tight. "It's personal when a deal is on the brink of falling through and the principals don't trust me to help them sort through it. They know I'm good with numbers and documents and spreadsheets and data, but they don't trust me when the chips are down."

I don't know what she says in response, but he says, "I

can fix this." Then, again, "I can fix this. Get MegaStar in the conference room, Monday morning at nine."

He paces.

"I'll be there."

He hangs up the phone.

"Bad?" I ask, trying to read the situation on his face.

"Not great," he admits. "The buyer found something."

"Something you can tell me about?"

"In vague terms. The seller was threatened at one point, a year or two back, with an intellectual property lawsuit. It didn't go to trial, but the information wasn't disclosed to the buyer, so now it's—a thing."

I wince.

"Yeah," he agrees. There's a tautness to his expression I can't read, and it makes my stomach hurt.

"You have to fly back tomorrow?"

"Yeah. But I can probably come back again. Do the rest of the due diligence here."

Probably. He doesn't sound confident, and he looks miserable. "It's okay if you can't," I say. "We knew you were going to have to leave at some point. And you'll...visit."

But it hits me how uncertain all of this is. He's about to get a promotion that will undoubtedly change the nature of his work life. I don't know much about the investment-bank food chain, but I have to imagine that the higher up you are, the more of your work involves face-to-face meetings and skin-on-skin handshakes. The promotion could make it harder to leave New York than he's planned for.

People who are away from their real lives have fantasies that don't fit their day-to-day realities and make promises they can't keep. Something that seems fun when you're thousands of miles from home might seem impossible when you're back on your own turf.

"You okay?" he asks.

For a second I think about lying about it, saying yes, but Preston and I have always been honest with each other, and I don't want to stop now.

"I'm scared," I confess. "That you'll get back there, and...this whole thing will feel like something that happened to you in another life. That this—that I—won't make any sense to you. That you'll want someone more serious. More like you."

He's shaking his head. "I don't want someone more serious," he says. "I want *you*. But I'm scared, too. I'm scared that what happened with Kali will happen again. That I'll go back, and after all this, after—"

He makes a gesture that encompasses us. And the festival. And maybe all of Rush Creek.

"—I won't be any different at all. I'll slip back into spending all my time working, and I won't know how to be there for you when you need me to, and—"

I don't know how to reassure myself, but I know how to reassure him. "That won't happen," I say. "I won't let you forget how to be there for me."

His eyes are dark and uncertain. "Promise?"

It makes me smile, and I reach for his hand. "If you promise you won't get back there and forget all about how good this is. Or decide your ideal woman is someone who works in I-banking and wears pencil skirts."

"Not a chance," he says fiercely, and then we're kissing, desperate and messy, like it's the last time.

When he finally breaks it off, he smiles down at me. "We should get this stuff unloaded," he says. "And then we have just enough time before the party at Hanna's to—"

I'm climbing up into the truck before he can finish the thought, and it makes him laugh—a rusty, beautiful, rarely used sound I can't get enough of.

41

———

PRESTON

I watch Natalie across the room—laughing with Hanna, Sonya, Ivy, elbowing my brother Shane, who has doubtless said something outrageous to her, kneeling to play puppets with Eloise, who is sitting on the couch with Saucy Cat on her hand. Natalie barks and makes Mr. Dog give Saucy Cat a kiss. She laughs, and even from across the room, I can hear the musical glitter of it, feel it in my bones. She looks up and sees me watching her, and she gives me a different kind of smile. Private, secret. Something curls, warm and sweet in my bloodstream.

I can still feel some of the lazy warmth left behind by our lovemaking earlier, but it's wrapped up with the chill of knowing it might be the last time...for a while.

The last time I left Rush Creek—at twenty-two—I basically surfed out on a wave of rage and self-righteousness. I was so sure that Kali was what I wanted, so sure that my grandfather was wrong about her and me. I was so sure I knew what I wanted: to go with my amazing artist girlfriend to New York City, marry her, and live happily ever after.

But this time, what I want feels...hazy.

Part of me is already back in New York, trying to figure out how the hell I'm going to save my deal and my promotion. How the hell I'm going to smooth over PowerFun's big failure of disclosure. Minimize it enough that MegaStar doesn't see it as a liability, convince the MegaStar stakeholders that one little hiccup shouldn't tank the perfect acquisition.

Because if I fail, everything I've worked for all these years goes straight to hell.

But meanwhile, my amazing girlfriend is right here, with a dog puppet on her hand, throwing back her head to laugh again. And even though Natalie did everything she could to reassure me earlier, she can't make certain fundamental truths go away.

You can't be all things to all people. While I was busy fulfilling the will, saving the land, and burying myself as deep as humanly possible in Natalie, things fell apart in New York.

When I go back to New York...

Even with Natalie's brave promise, I don't know yet if I can be what Grantham-Hoyer needs from me and what I want to give her at the same time.

I drift like a ghost through the party, accepting congratulations from my brothers, Sonya, Ivy, Sonya's friends. A few of the Rush Creek firefighters are there because apparently Sonya's friend Reggie is now engaged to a firefighter named Ford, and his friends are becoming her friends.

Weggers is there because he invited himself, and Nan is there because her grandson is one of the firefighters.

My gaze finds Natalie again. She's taken Eloise into her lap and now has both puppets on her hands, working them in conversation I can't hear. Her head bends toward Eloise's soft hair, her nose almost touching it. My chest tightens so much it hurts.

"You're really leaving, huh?"

Shane has joined me, his shoulder nudging me, his eyes following mine.

I nod, forcing myself to look away from Natalie.

"And she's not going with you." He nods in her direction.

"She belongs here," I say.

"And you—belong in New York?" he asks.

"It's who I am," I say.

He tilts his head to one side. "I'd be more inclined to say, *It's what you do.*"

"Isn't it the same thing?"

Shane shakes his head. "Not usually." He's quiet for a moment, and I think he's done, but then he says, "It's okay to stick to your guns. But do it for your own reasons."

I give him a sharp look. "What makes you think I haven't?"

He shrugs. "It was a guess. I don't know exactly what went down between you and Grandfather, but knowing you both, everyone probably got extra stubborn and dug in. I've always figured you stuck New York out as long as you did because the idea of slinking home wasn't terribly appealing."

"Maybe I stuck New York out because I love finance," I say.

He gives me a sidelong glance. "You love problem-solving. You love challenges. Maybe you even love numbers. But finance?"

"What do you know about what I love?"

I expect laughter or mocking, but Shane just sighs. "You'd be surprised," he says. "Don't forget, it's my job to get inside other people's heads and understand what makes them tick."

"Yeah, well—don't flatter yourself."

Still, he's looking at me with such steady affection, I sigh and say, "I wanted to show him he was wrong."

"About what?"

"That I couldn't make it in New York. That Kali and I weren't in it for the long haul."

"Well," Shane says. "One for two isn't bad." He raises his eyebrows. "You know it doesn't matter what he thinks, right? One, he was kind of a dick."

I snort.

"And two, he's actually...dead."

For some reason, that makes us both laugh really hard. We're still laughing when Hanna comes up to me with Eloise in her arms.

"Pres," she says. "I'm about to put El to bed. Want to say goodbye to her? You're leaving super early tomorrow, right?"

"Right," I say and take Eloise from her. Eloise reaches out and boops my nose. I taught her to do that, and my eyes sting a little, even though I'll be back. Soon. "If she learns anything new while I'm gone, text me," I say.

"Like *anything*?" Hanna asks suspiciously. "Like, if she learns to like a new food?"

"Anything *fun*," I say. "Like nose booping."

Eloise boops my nose again, for good measure.

"Bye-bye, Eloise," I say.

"Buh-duh, Padda," she says back.

I freeze. "Did she just say my *name*?"

"I think she did," Hanna says, delighted. "She's never done that before. Preston," she says to Eloise.

"Padda," Eloise says and boops my nose again.

I turn away so neither Hanna nor Eloise sees the tears shining in my eyes.

42

PRESTON

"It's not the lawsuit itself that concerns me," says Thompson Merraker, the CEO of MegaStar. "It's the fact that PowerFun chose not to disclose it."

Anjali shoots me a look from the other side of the conference table. It says, *I know you're distracted. I don't know why you're so distracted, but I don't care. You need to pull yourself together and fix this.*

She's right. I can't be two places—geographically or mentally—at once. I've proven that to myself over and over again.

I need to get my act together and save this situation.

What would Preston Hott do if he were here?

Excellent question, Preston. Good talk.

I square my shoulders. Take a breath. Steel myself. "I understand your concern." I put both hands on the table, to the sides of my shoulders. Lean forward. "I've had a long conversation with Julie Ambrose"—that's the PowerFun CEO—"and she understands your concern, too. What she told me is that they regarded the lawsuit as such a nonissue that it literally didn't occur to them that they might need to bring it up. But she also intends, going forward, to be much more cognizant of raising issues, even if she can't see the immediate significance of them."

I feel weary. I wish adults were like kids, that you could boop them on the nose and make everything okay. I wish they could get outside the narrow scope of their obsessions and see that while they're locked in this conference room arguing about things that almost certainly don't matter, there are people outside eating cake and jumping on trampolines and tagging each other with Nerf darts.

Maybe those people are the ones who actually know what matters.

"I genuinely believe Julie was acting in the best faith," I tell Thompson and the other MegaStar C-suite execs. "That this was a slipup, that it won't happen again, and that it doesn't affect the valuation of PowerFun. I think you should go forward with the deal—and you have to believe that I wouldn't say that if I didn't feel it in my soul. I'm not in this business to pull the wool over anyone's eyes. I'm in this business to make the best possible deals for everyone concerned."

I can feel the mood shifting in my favor. There's a murmur among the MegaStar execs. Their COO, Tanya Sabershaaf, whispers something to Thompson.

Anjali gives me a *good job* look, and I wait to feel something, a sense of accomplishment—anything, but mostly I want to get back into bed beside Natalie and eat one of the breakfast sandwiches from Morning Rush. And maybe one of Carol's chocolate croissants (sorry, Nan).

I want my day to be over so I can sit with Natalie in the dining room at Hott Springs Eternal and tell her about it.

At the very least, I want to call her and hear her voice.

It doesn't feel like nearly enough, but I still crave it.

Thankfully, Thompson pushes his chair back and says, "We trust you, Preston. If that's what you see here, then that's enough for us. Let's finish up the due diligence and get this deal signed."

The C-suiters head out, leaving Anjali and me alone.

"Good work, Preston," she says. "And thanks for coming back here so quickly."

"I'll always do what needs to be done," I say. "You know that."

"I do know that. And I think the board and the other directors will take this as evidence of that, too. I hope it hasn't caused trouble for you with your situation at home."

I shake my head. "No. Things are settled there."

But they don't feel settled. Not really. They feel unfinished. Like I've left the oven on and gone for a trip.

"Excellent," she says.

I turn to go.

"Pres," she says.

I turn back.

"Whatever it is, put it out of your head. You're almost there. And you need to focus all your attention on getting there. You almost lost that one. You pulled it out, but it might not be that easy next time. I want your head in the game and your eyes on the prize. This isn't just about you, you know. My reputation is staked on you. That's not nothing."

"No," I say. "No. That's not nothing at all. I appreciate it more than you know. It means an enormous amount to me."

"And if you ink this deal," she says, and her voice is surprisingly tender for a woman who told me she's been called an ice queen on multiple occasions, "you'll have everything you ever wanted. You've told me that yourself."

"Right," I say. "Right."

I have. And it's true.

Or it *was* true.

43

NATALIE

8:00 A.M. PDT

Thinking of you. Did you sort everything out with your deal?

12:13 P.M. PDT

Sorry, was still in the meeting. Yes, sorted things out. Shit, gotta go

2:11 P.M. PDT

Everything okay?

3:15 P.M. PDT

3:47 P.M. PDT

Sorry, things got a little hairy again. Maybe we can try to talk once I'm home.

That would be awesome.

I'll call you.

4:25 P.M. PDT

I'm sorry—haven't left yet. Some stuff came up.

No worries! Time zones are in our favor.

5:41 P.M. PDT

Think it's going to be around 8:30 your time by the time I can call.

Geez—are you really going to be there till 11:30?

Looks like it. I'm so sorry.

The first Wedding Launch is tonight, so— why don't I call you when I get back from that?

Perfect.

9:27 P.M. PDT

Okay, I'm back. You up?

7:19 A.M. PDT

God! I'm so sorry. I came home and lay down on the couch with my phone and the next thing I knew it was morning. I didn't want to text and wake you up.

7:34 A.M. PDT

It's okay! I get it. Can you talk now?

I call his office line, because he gave me the number in case I needed it.

A man answers.

"Franklin?" I ask.

"And who would this be, pray tell?"

"This is Natalie."

There's a long silence. Then Franklin says, "Natalie. Would you by any chance happen to be a big fan of Italian pastry?"

"That's me," I say.

"Did you like the food?"

"I loved it! Thank you so much!"

"Don't thank me," he says. "I was paid generously for my time. It's just nice to see Preston doing something that isn't work."

"Speaking of Preston, any chance you can squeeze me into his schedule?"

"That implies that he has a schedule, other than 'respond to the latest crisis.' He's in a meeting right now," Franklin says. "But I can have him call you when he gets out."

"That would be awesome."

1:09 P.M. PDT

Can I call you now?

3:04 P.M. PDT

Damn, sorry, was running body painting. I could call you now?

6:32 P.M. PDT

Are you still at work?

9:42 P.M. PDT

Preston? I'm heading to bed. Miss you. Good night!

10:14 P.M. PDT

I'm so sorry—I'm going to try to come home this weekend to see you—

7:19 A.M. PDT

That would be amazing.

8:03 A.M. PDT

Scratch that. New crisis. But the weekend after. I swear. I'm so, so sorry Natalie.

44

PRESTON

"**A**nnabel Sweet wants a face-to-face with you," Franklin says into my ear three days later when I pick up the phone.

Dread coils in the pit of my stomach. Annabel Sweet represents PowerFun's CEO, Julie Ambrose, as the banker on the seller's side. She works for a different I-banking firm. An out-of-the-blue call is not a good sign.

I've worked fifty-six of the last seventy-two hours. Slept eleven.

It's just as well. I don't want to spend any time in my apartment. It's too big and empty.

There's a huge living room that could probably seat twenty, easily, if there were any furniture left in it besides an ugly, hard gray couch and a matching gray armchair. Kali took the rest.

The walls are white, and the decor is bachelor chic. The kind of art you buy from a decorator, that's made to fill space and add color and maybe even provoke discussion. Kali took all the art that was really art, because she'd chosen it all to begin with. Sculptures and paintings, vivid and imaginative. What's left is a mockery of art.

The kitchen is huge, black and white, stark lines and cold surfaces. No one has cooked in it since Kali left.

She took the pottery that her artist friends had thrown. The glass bowls they'd blown. The dish towels they'd woven and screen printed.

What's left is open and cold and arid.

I'd rather be here, where at least Franklin gets paid to keep me company.

"Can I set up a Zoom for you and Annabel?" he asks.

"Sure," I say.

I click into the Zoom Franklin has set up. Annabel's in there, looking grim in a way that does nothing for my stomach.

"What's up?" I ask her.

"My seller has cold feet."

"Warm them up for her."

"Preston, this isn't a joke. You know she's had serious reservations about culture clash all along, but the due diligence dragging on so long has given her even more time to worry about it. She's saying it's a little like AT&T buying Pixar."

"AT&T didn't buy Pixar."

At some point in the last few days, I settled back into this version of myself. The old version. Recognizable. Cool, hard, ruthless. I like this self better; he's got more armor. He doesn't have time to second-guess himself or think about how much he misses Natalie. He only has the bandwidth for what's happening here and now in this office.

"I think that's her whole point," Annabel says darkly.

"She didn't love the way MegaStar handled themselves during due diligence. She hasn't liked what she's seen during site visits. She thinks MegaStar will crush Power-Fun's soul. And every time she's tried to approach Thompson to raise concerns, he's said the equivalent of 'What culture?'"

I groan. "Thompson."

"I know," Annabel grumbles. She doesn't want this thing to fall apart any more than I do. She's invested just as much for just as long in its success.

Now she sighs. "You told me when we started this process that you believe the most important thing in a good acquisition was fit."

I fidget with a pile of folders on my desk, adjusting the corners so they line up perfectly. "I still believe that. And I still believe this is the right fit. I think Thompson, for all his faults, sees clearly what's good in PowerFun."

"Then he's going to have to find some way to show that to Julie," Annabel says. "Because otherwise she's going to walk away from this deal."

Annabel, having delivered that zinger, brings the meeting to a close, leaving me feeling sick to my stomach.

Franklin comes in. "Annabel wanting a meeting out of the blue can't be good, can it?"

"Nope," I say. "PowerFun is worried about culture match. Julie Ambrose has, in Annabel's words, cold feet."

"Shit," he says.

"I need something. Something big. Something that will convince PowerFun that Thompson Merraker and Mega-Star genuinely have the company's best interest at heart. That they won't gut PowerFun and fire all its employees.

That they understand PowerFun's vision and want to make it a reality on a bigger scale."

"Oh, only that?" Franklin asks dryly.

"This is so not my strong suit," I say with a groan.

Natalie would be so much better at this.

Natalie would know what to do.

What would Natalie do?

Natalie Natalie Natalie Natalie Natalie.

Dancing on the desk, holding on to my tie, wielding a sledgehammer, glistening wet in a bikini, bouncing on a trampoline, eating cake, under me with her face slack with pleasure, on top of me in a pool of Jell-O—

And I'm here...doing...what?

"Preston," Franklin says, waving a hand in front of my face. "This is absolutely your strong suit. You do this in your sleep. With one hand tied behind your back. What *happened* to you in Rush Creek? And don't tell me *nothing* because I drove to New Haven and then flew across the country to get you *pastries.* You've never even made me go to Brooklyn for takeout. Plus, that was enough food for a small army. Don't tell me you just had a hankering for Italian."

"Shit," I groan.

"Don't worry," he says. "I won't tell anyone. But—who is this *Natalie?*"

He says it with a ridiculous French accent.

"Nobody," I say.

"She's definitely not nobody," he says. "You know how I know? Because you are a fucking mess. And in all the time I've known you, I have *never* seen you not one hundred percent on top of things."

I sigh. There's not much point in lying to the guy whose job it is to watch you like a hawk and meet your every need.

"Yeah," I say. "She's not nobody. She's—"

And then, because I think, despite my best intentions, Franklin is my *friend*, I tell him. Just a little bit. About how the first time Natalie and I met, it was in Hanna's office and I tried to fire her and the second time we met, she was dancing on a desk. I tell him about Jell-O wrestling and smashing things with baseball bats and sledgehammers and about Operation Fun.

"I don't want to fuck this up," I say when I bring him up to the present moment. "And I'm already fucking it up. It's been less than a week, and work is eating me alive, and she and I are like ships in the night. And I knew this was going to happen because I fucked things up with Kali."

"Whoa," Franklin says. "Hang on. Hold your horses. You're one of *Newer York*'s titans of finance. You should know that *past performance is no guarantee of future results*."

I stare at him, confused.

"Right? Isn't that the saying?"

"Yeah, but—"

"Well, it works both ways, right? You're not necessarily going to get rich this time because you got rich last time. *And* just because you fucked things up with Kali doesn't mean you're going to fuck things up with Natalie." He gives me a sharp look. "I'm your assistant, right?"

"Right."

"It's my job to know everything about you. Where you want me to order lunch from, whether you like your pants pressed with a crease or not, which hand you hold your dick with when you take a piss—"

I close my eyes and wave that off. "Jesus, Franklin—"

He shrugs. "My point being I've *never* seen you not get something you want. You're the hardest working, most focused person I know, and if you tell me you don't want to fuck things up with Natalie?" He gives a decisive nod. "You're not going to fuck them up."

My forehead feels too tight. My hands and feet are hot.

Because he's right, of course. He knows me.

And he's telling me, as someone who knows me—

That I've got this.

It's going to be okay.

Natalie and I—we're going to make this work.

And it's the best news I've ever heard.

Better than a promotion, for fucking sure.

He crosses his arms, not waiting for a response from me. "But as the guy who *really* wants to keep his job, can I suggest we tackle the other problem first? Because as much as I want you to live happily ever after, my personal interest lies much more with your professional success. Can we solve the PowerFun/MegaStar problem and *then* figure out how not to fuck things up with *Natalie*? How about I get you a coffee? While you pull your head out of your ass and try to figure out how to keep PowerFun from wrecking their own deal?"

Grateful, I say, "Americano. Black."

"You know, you could shake it up every once in a while. Just to keep things interesting for me."

I'm about to say *nah*, but then it's my turn to shrug. "Sure," I say. "Bring me something different."

"You're letting me choose?"

"Yeah," I say. "Surprise me."

At the door, Franklin hesitates. "I know I'm just an executive assistant," he says, "but if there's anything I can do to help, you'll let me know, won't you?"

I sigh. "Not sure there's much," I say. "Unless you can convince the most uptight guy in business to loosen up enough to prove that he understands the concept of fun."

Franklin's eyebrows go up so far so fast I'm afraid they're going to tangle in his hair.

It takes me a minute to hear what I've said.

What would Natalie do?

I know *exactly* what Natalie would do.

"Right," I say. "Okay. Bring me that coffee, and then get ready to take some notes because I know how we're gonna fix this."

45

NATALIE

As soon as the festival ends, Hott Springs Eternal inaugurates its first few activities—the Wedding Launch, flower arranging, Wine and Paint night, and the ever-popular Jell-O wrestling and Nerf battle. They're all a resounding success. We're deep into wedding season now, and the sign-ups are filled almost instantly, with waiting lists forming for all the activities. Everything goes as smoothly as can be expected (we won't talk about the paint I can't *quite* get out of the HSE dining room floor; I'm working on better floor coverings for the next round), and I feel...

Mostly empty.

Because the person I most want to share my success with isn't here.

I have hundreds of photos of people enjoying our offerings, some of which I posted to social media, but most of which I just page through, wishing I could text them to Preston but not wanting to deluge him with texts I know he doesn't have the time to respond to right now.

Especially the one of Hanna looking down at the world's most half-assed flower arrangement. (*That's why I hire people to do that part,* she said grumpily as I took the photo.)

Impetuously, I send him the photo, captioned with Hanna's grumpy utterance.

And wait.

And wait.

Our communication has been painfully spotty this whole week. But this is the first time he's completely ignored me—and as much as I'd like to be impervious, I'm not. I'm hurt.

After a while I get sick of waiting by the phone for a guy who clearly doesn't have time for me, and I decide to celebrate my successes without him.

Classic rewards include chocolate, wine, and spa visits.

Which is why I'm dressed in my robe and headed down to the hot springs, in defiance of every portion of my soul telling me to stay away from the scene of the crime.

Preston may not remember I exist, but I'm not going to let that deprive me of the chance to have a hot dip.

Except as I approach the hot springs, I hear voices.

I stop. I don't want to interrupt anyone else's intimate evening. Personal experience has taught me that what goes on at night at Hott Springs Eternal isn't an open house.

"Natalie!" a voice says happily behind me, and I turn to find Reggie from the spa. She's balancing a plate of cookies on a box of wine. "Can you get that gate for me?"

Obligingly, I do.

"Can you grab the cookies from me and put them on

that table?" she asks, tipping her head to indicate the table in question.

I do. I can see who's in the water now—Sonya and Ivy.

"I brought a buddy," Reggie says.

I open my mouth to say that I don't want to butt in, that I can come back another night, but Sonya beams delightedly at me.

"Natalie!" she says. "We were doing some planning for Ivy's two weddings, and then we got burned out and decided to quit for the night and have a dip instead."

"Two weddings?" I ask, raising my eyebrow at Ivy.

"One for our actual friends and family, and one for Shane's screaming public," Ivy says, rolling her eyes.

"She's just being modest," Sonya says. "It's her screaming public, too."

"It's all the people shipping me and Shane, basically," Ivy says. "Anyway, we're not actually planning both. Publicists are planning one and we're"—she gestures at her friends—"planning the other one." She looks to me. "Do you know the whole story?"

"I know the gist," I say.

"I should fill in the details, right?" Sonya says.

"If she has all night," Ivy says, but before I can try again to extricate myself gracefully, Sonya has jumped in to tell me how Ivy and Shane got themselves into their now famous—and maybe slightly infamous—celebrity match.

Reggie has been pouring glasses of wine while Sonya talks, and she starts handing them around. She puts one in my hand.

"I—"

"Come on in," Sonya says.

"I don't want to crash your party," I finally manage.

"Don't be ridiculous," Ivy says. "You're always welcome. You're one of us now."

I duck my chin.

"What?" Sonya asks.

"I don't know if it's going to work," I admit. "He more or less warned me it wouldn't. Couldn't. The day before he left. He told me he was scared that he couldn't change and that once he was back in New York, he would slip back into spending all his time working and wouldn't have time for me. And like a dope, I said, 'I won't let that happen.' Like it was something I'd have any control over. And now he's doing exactly what he said he was afraid of." I bite my lip.

Ivy and Sonya exchange a look.

"You know," Sonya says, so casually that I can tell she's not. "Quinn and I broke up for a little while. After we fulfilled the terms of the will. Because we didn't think we could make it work."

"And so did Shane and I," Ivy says. "For the same reason."

I know what they're trying to do, and I appreciate it—but I don't want to get anyone's hopes up about this—including mine. I shake my head. "I think this might be a different situation," I say. "I think I was a fun diversion for him while he was here, but—maybe that's all it was."

Ivy's quiet for a moment. Then she says, "It doesn't matter, you know. To us. Whether you end up with him or not. Once you've been through the Hott will wringer, you're part of the family forever. You can't get rid of us. You're stuck with us. So you might as well get in and enjoy the water." And she reaches up to take my wineglass so I can climb in.

I hesitate a moment. But the water steams temptingly, and their faces are all soft, smiling, and sympathetic. I lower myself in.

"To Fox Hott and his worst impulses," Sonya says with a sigh, and Ivy hands me my glass as she and Reggie lift theirs.

So do I. We clink, and I recognize that the tightness in my chest now isn't sadness. It's something else entirely.

Belonging to this little group feels a lot like sinking into the soothing embrace of the hot springs.

46

PRESTON

"You're a dead man!" bellows Thompson Merraker, closing in on one of PowerFun's marketing people, brandishing his laser blaster. The marketer goes down, having taken his last hit.

"Who's next?!" Thompson cries. "Who's the next dead man walking!?" He waves his blaster around like a deranged Stormtrooper.

From behind a foam obstacle, Julie Ambrose rises like a phoenix. "I. Am. No. Man!" she war cries, tearing off a series of blasts and pinning Thompson with his last hit.

He staggers, clutches his chest. He waves his fist at the sky and curses his misfortune. Then he goes down.

I've never seen him like this. In fact, I've never seen him in anything other than a suit and tie, buttoned up and deadly serious.

And this?

This is perfect.

Julie stands over her kill, crowing. "Vanquished!"

"Fair and square," Thompson concedes, rising to kneeling and reaching out a hand to shake hers.

They're both grinning.

They come to the side of the arena, where I'm standing, grinning myself.

"This was so fun," Thompson says. "I haven't had fun like this..."

"Since you were a kid?" I ask him.

"For a long time," he admits. "Way longer than I want to think about. And what a great way to—ease tensions."

Julie leans on the railing on my other side. "Smart move," she says to me. "I don't think anything you could've told me about Thompson's capacity to be human would have gotten through to me."

"Hey," Thompson says lightly. "Go easy on your new coworker."

She raises her eyebrows.

"Okay," he concedes. "I have been accused of being an android before. But I do think PowerFun has a great business model, and to the extent it's possible for us to let your culture percolate through ours—I think we'd benefit greatly from it."

He sounds like an android again, but it's a lot easier in this context to see that it's a kind of awkward stiffness, not an inherent lack of soul. I hope Julie sees it too...and her wry smile in my direction tells me she probably does.

"Let me take your team out to dinner," Thompson says.

Julie looks startled. "Um, sure," she says.

"No business talk," I warn them. "Or at least no promises you don't know if you can keep."

"Come with us," Thompson says.

"I'd love to," I say, "but I have work to do."

I'M EXHAUSTED by the time I get back to my apartment. My talk with Anjali went a lot longer than I thought it would. It's almost ten.

The last thing I'm expecting—or wanting—when I open the door is to see Shane, Quinn, and Rhys sitting on my couch.

"What the fuck are you doing here?" I ask.

"Staging an intervention," Shane says.

"I'm not," Rhys says. "I'm only here because they asked me to be here."

"I don't need an intervention," I say.

"No, you really, really do," Shane says.

I look at Quinn, hoping he's prepared to be the saner of the two of them. But he just nods. "You do."

"The thing is," Shane says, "I know you think we're full of shit, but there's something to the grandfather matchmaking thing. And we're not just saying that because it happened to work twice. We're saying it because we saw you with Natalie, and it was—" He stops.

"You were—" Quinn attempts.

They both stare at me like I'm supposed to know what they're saying.

"We think you should come back to Rush Creek and tell her you're in love with her," Shane says.

I snort. "You're too late."

Rhys lets out a deep sigh of relief. "I'm so fucking glad to hear you say that," he says. "You can save yourself so much time and money by never getting married in the first place and never having to get divorced."

Shane and Quinn glare at him.

"Don't say it's too late!" Shane says. "It's never too late! It's never too late to realize that you've been a tool and a dick. You can tell her you never should have put all that energy into trying to prove shit to Granddad and that you're all done. You're letting it go and you want to be with her."

"No," I say, "I *know*. I get all that. I mean you're too late to convince me to try to make things work with Natalie."

"She's so great, Pres—you can't mean that," Quinn says, and it's Quinn, man of few words and fewer big emotions, so that means a lot coming from him.

"No," I say again, because why is it so hard sometimes for two people to have a conversation about the same thing? "I mean you're too late to convince me because I already had my big revelation. Probably while you were in the air over the Midwest. I already gave notice to my boss."

"You—what?" Quinn and Shane say simultaneously, even though I've just, as far as I can tell, done exactly what they were trying to convince me to do.

Rhys shakes his head in disgust.

"I had this big come-to-Jesus moment about how the best mergers are between the most unlikely companies— you know, opposites attract and all that—quit my job, put my apartment on the market, and I'm moving back to Rush Creek."

"Oh," Quinn and Shane say and exchange a glance.

"That was an expensive trip for nothing," I say sympathetically.

Rhys glares at both my other brothers. "Told you," he says.

"Yeah," Quinn tells him, "but you were wrong about everything else."

Shane shrugs. "Any chance you have any expensive Scotch?" he asks.

"Of course," I say. "And in fairness, the trip wasn't totally for nothing. I have something I need you to do. ASAP."

47

NATALIE

The morning after my dip in the hot springs with Sonya, Ivy, and Reggie, I go out for a bagel and coffee and come back to find my mother's car parked next to mine. I get out of my car, hoping it's a hallucination, but she gets out of hers, too, and walks around to greet me.

Or, really, scowl at me.

"You might have mentioned that you and Lloyd are no longer a couple."

I bite my lip and say, "Hi, Mom."

She rubs her fingertips over her forehead. She's wearing a knee-length gray skirt and a seafoam blouse, and my eye catches on a small bleach stain on the skirt. I wonder if she knows it's there. I bet she doesn't. She wouldn't have worn it if she did.

"It was awkward, finding out the way I did. I ran into him at Target, and I started toward him with the intention of giving him a big hug. He got an uncomfortable look on his face. And then a woman stepped around the corner and cozied up to him, someone named—" She searches her memory.

"Susie," I finish, wincing. As frustrating as my mother is, she didn't deserve to be blindsided. "I'm sorry I didn't give you a heads-up."

"I'm sure you had your reasons," she says in a tone that suggests exactly the opposite.

"I didn't want to tell you about it the other night at dinner, with everyone around."

"You could have called me and told me."

I could have. But I knew how much she liked him. I knew how disappointed she'd be.

And I knew she'd make it my fault.

"I liked him for you," she says. "This is what I worried about. That he would get tired of waiting for you to pull your life together."

Wait a second.

Wait a fucking second.

How did Lloyd's being an asshole become about me and whether I, quote, unquote, "have my life together?"

"That's not what happened." My voice surprises me. It's firm and sure. The way I feel when I'm running an activity. "He was seeing someone else. I caught him holding hands with her in a coffee shop."

She flinches at that. "That's...unfortunate," she says, as though Lloyd's betrayal was an accident of fate and not a decision he made. "He was good for you."

"No," I say. "He wasn't. He didn't know me. Or want to know me. He didn't understand what makes me tick."

"What *does* make you tick, Natalie? Because I'm not sure I know, either. And to be honest, I'm not sure *you* know."

Two weeks ago, those words would have crawled into my chest and burrowed in, a dark knot of self-doubt, like rot in fruit. Right now, though, it's like I'm wearing a face guard and the chest plate and swinging a baseball bat at an old VCR: the sharp, bright clarity of anger. And something else. Confidence.

"You're wrong," I say. "I do know." I'm thinking of Preston again. Thinking of how it felt to make him smile. To make him laugh. To watch him flip himself into the foam pit. "I know exactly what makes me tick."

She's visibly startled, and so am I because surely, this can't be the first time I've pushed back. Stood up to her.

Except her expression suggests it is. Have I always just accepted whatever she wants me to believe about myself?

Well, I think, *enough of that.*

I don't stomp my foot or even cross my arms, but I do straighten up a little. I point. I say, "You have a little something on your skirt. Right *there.*"

Her gaze dips to the smudge, then comes back up again, steely, to fix on me. "You're awfully smug for someone who's been unemployed for months—"

"I'm employed now."

"—who's lost the relationship you were in—"

Nope. "I didn't *lose* it. He ruined it."

She refuses to acknowledge that. "—who's living in a hotel room—"

I cross my arms. Plant my feet. It feels good. "I have company housing."

"You have a temporary job."

"I have a *great* job." Each time I push back, I feel a little stronger.

"A job isn't a career."

It's a thing my mother has said to me a hundred times since I bailed out of communications.

"No, but it could be," I tell her.

She frowns. The lines at the sides of her mouth are deep. "There's a difference between stringing jobs together and having a career."

"There is a difference," I agree. "The difference is your attitude toward what you're doing. Any job can become a career if you're good at it and love it. Activities coordinator is my job." I take a deep breath and echo what Preston said to her outside my room the other day. "*Bringing people joy* is my career."

For a second I think I've gotten through to her. She hesitates. She looks, just a little, thoughtful. Then her frown deepens. "Please tell me you're not losing focus on going back to school."

I think about all the brochures stuffed into a pocket of my suitcase. All the websites she sent me links to.

I think about the Wilder brothers with nail polish on their fingers. I think about Preston Hott in a pit of purple Jell-O. I think about the Wilder and Hott kids blasting Nerf darts at each other.

"I'm not going back to school."

I didn't know for sure it was true until I said it out loud, but I should have.

What I wanted, all this time, was to be who she wanted me to be.

What I want now is to be me.

I guess Preston isn't the only one who needed permission to let go of who they thought they were.

"Natalie," she warns.

"Mom," I say back.

We stare each other down. I don't look away. Not this time.

I think about Ivy and Sonya and Reggie, who told me that I'm welcome in their world regardless of whether Preston and I end up together.

I think of Preston, who told me that my mother wasn't fair to me. Who told my mother that I brought people joy and then told me that I was funny and generous and giving and *fun*.

Preston knows exactly who I am.

Even if he's never said the words, he loves me for it.

I know what that feels like.

I don't have to settle for less.

"I have a job I love that I'm good at," I tell my mother. "I know it's not what you want to do with your life, and you've made it abundantly clear that it's not what you want me to do with my life. But I'm the only person who knows what makes me happy."

I hear my own words then, and everything shifts into sharp relief.

"I gotta go," I say, and then I'm running toward the lodge.

48

NATALIE

The closer I get to my room, the more conviction I have about what I want to do next.

Except when I get there, Sonya, Ivy, and Reggie are standing in front of the door.

"What is this?" I ask. "An intervention?"

"No," Sonya says at the same time Ivy says, "Yes," and Reggie says, "Not exactly, but—"

They all clamp their mouth shut.

"We want to take you somewhere special. To celebrate. You know. The first week of—events."

"I can't," I say, reaching past Ivy to unlock my door and push inside.

"You can," she says.

They follow me in without waiting for an invitation.

"Natalie," Sonya says to my back as I pull my small suitcase from the closet, toss it onto the bed, and begin filling it haphazardly with my stuff. "You want to come with us."

"You don't *want* me to come with you," I tell her. "You

want me to pack this suitcase, go to New York, and tell Preston how I feel about him."

All three of their mouths fall open.

"Don't look so surprised," I say sternly. "You knew this was coming, didn't you?"

Ivy winces. "We might have...thought..."

"No," Sonya says. "I mean, I hoped it was. I'd never seen Preston smile before you two started working together. If you'd told me I'd watch Preston wield a Nerf blaster and yell, 'Yippee-ki-yay,' I would have laughed my ass off. So I was rooting for you two. But I'd be lying if I said I thought the writing was on the wall. Relationships are way more complicated than that. And he does live in New York."

"Yeah," I say. "I don't know if I can convince him to give this a shot."

They exchange another glance.

"I think you can," Sonya says. "I really do. But...before you do that, come with us to do this...thing...and then if you still think you need to go to New York, we'll drive you to the airport."

"What kind of thing?" I ask, cocking my head because now that I've decided to put everything on the line, I want to get it over with. In case he says no. Which he probably will, despite Sonya's optimism. He'll probably take one look at me and pat me kindly on the head and go back to whatever spreadsheet he's making.

Another round of looks. "It's like a—"

"A *concert*," Ivy says.

Sonya frowns.

"You got me Taylor Swift tickets!" I tease.

"I *wish*," Sonya breathes. "No. Don't get your hopes up for anything like that. Nothing, you know, huge or expensive. Just—we wanted to do something nice for you. And...we're going to do your hair and makeup. For the concert-thing."

"Concert-thing," I repeat, eyes narrowing. "Come on, guys, what's going on?"

"Can't answer that," Reggie says, giving a steely look to her friends. "Go. Get in the shower, wet your hair, and plant your ass in this chair." She indicates the desk chair.

My eyes narrow. "You don't think I can do my own hair and makeup?"

"You're going to turn down the opportunity to have it done by trained professionals?" Reggie asks.

"For a 'concert-thing'?" I tease.

"This isn't just any 'concert-thing,'" Ivy says. "Take my word for it. You want the full treatment."

Which is why, a few minutes later, having swiftly showered, I'm sitting in a hotel desk chair having my hair and makeup done by my friends, trying to guess where they're taking me.

"Is it one of those picnic-in-the-park events?" I ask. There's a whole series on the Rush Creek green in the summer. Local bands play, and you can spread out a blanket or chairs and listen. It would definitely qualify as a concert-thing.

"Um," Ivy says. "Maybe more *thing* and less concert than that."

"Good, because I was starting to get afraid we were going to see one of those rock legends of the eighties performing live at the local casino."

"Hey," Reggie says grumpily. "There was good music in the eighties."

She's a little older than the three of us. Not old enough to have listened to a lot of music in the actual eighties, but old enough to have heard a lot more of it than the rest of us.

"You're not taking me to see *Hamilton*, right?" I ask.

"Nope," Sonya confirms. "Now stop trying to guess, because we're not going to tell you."

Reggie fusses over my face, and Sonya piles my curls on my head, and Ivy mopes over the meager contents of my closet, saying, "Seriously, Natalie, you own exactly one summer dress?" To which Reggie says, "We're fixing that first thing tomorrow."

49

NATALIE

When they're done dolling me up, Sonya, Ivy, and Reggie hustle me down in the elevator and out to the parking lot, where they blindfold me.

"What the hell?" I ask.

"Just—go with it," Reggie says.

"This concert-thing better be good."

"The best," Ivy says, and she sounds a little giddy.

We walk for a long time, but not a very long time, and then they guide me over a threshold and across a wood floor. And then Sonya says "Ta da!" and unties my blindfold.

I blink into the sudden light as my vision resolves

The whole Hott Springs Eternal barn has been done up as a kid's birthday party. Balloons, piñatas, streamers, colorful plates and napkins. And the room is full of people. I turn my head slowly, letting all the faces sink in. It's disorienting because the people—they're my people but from all different moments in my life. Two of my elementary school friends who I'm still in touch with on Facebook. A couple of my high school friends. Coworkers from the nursing home. Tons of Wilders and Hotts.

Then, stepping forward, an anchor in the storm: Preston. Tall, broad shouldered, wearing a pair of dress slacks and a button-down shirt and looking better than birthday cake.

Holding his hands out to me.

"You're invited," he says, "to a party just for you."

And I start to cry.

"Oh, God!" he says. "I'm sorry, Natalie. I thought—"

And as impulsively as Preston Hott ever does anything, he wraps me in his arms. Tight. Squeezing me. He's hard and muscular and warm and smells like him, and I cry harder.

"It's good crying," I manage through my tears. "I'm just very, very glad to see you—and what the fuck is this?"

"It's all your missing birthday parties," he says. "I wasn't sure which ones went missing, so I tried to do them all."

"Is this a grand gesture?" I whisper.

"Yeah," he says. "This—and also, I quit my job, and I sold my apartment—"

"You didn't have to do that!"

"Actually," he says, "I did. I kept that job way too long to prove something that didn't need proving."

"That you're amazing?"

His expression goes soft and warm at that, and he brushes a strand of hair back from my face. "That I can live the life *I* want to live," he says, bending to brush a kiss across my forehead. "In this particular case, what I *want* is to live with you in Rush Creek. And to get the chance to love you. I love you."

"That seems—like the important part," I say, choking up again. "I love you, too."

Things happen in a whirlwind after that. People are greeting me, some I haven't seen in years, hugging me, wishing me happy birthday, even though my birthday's three months away still. I'm pretty sure that's not the point. People bring me drinks—Hi-C in paper cups, root beer in plastic cups, beer in Solo cups. It turns out Preston wasn't kidding about all my missing birthday parties.

My mouth falls open when I see all the birthday cakes, representing all the stages of childhood.

"The Wilder kids helped," Preston says. "They told me what the right cakes would be."

There's a baby's first birthday cake, an Elmo cake, a pink princess cake, a horse cake, a tropical-themed cake, a plain chocolate cake with bright colored frosting—"for when you got too dignified as a teenager for themes," Preston explains. "Anna, Amanda's oldest, said that was a thing. And then this one is for you now."

It's a rainbow explosion, every color and type of sprinkles. "It's a *fuck that, definitely NOT better than sex with you* cake," Preston says, leaning close and whispering it against my ear, sending shivers all through my body and making me want to skip straight to the end of the party.

There are activities for every age, too—hide and seek, fishing in the kiddie pool, pin the tail on the donkey, treasure and scavenger hunts—and Preston and I do them all, and I keep sneaking looks at him because he's here and he loves me and he wants us to be together. I have no idea how we're going to make that happen, but I believe we will and that seems like the best not-birthday present ever.

As it turns out, there are lots of birthday gifts for me, too. Tickle Me Elmo and a matched set of Elsa and Anna dolls and an Easy-Bake Oven and a huge Lego set and a dumb phone and a fantastic upgrade to my beloved portable speaker. And then Preston says, "It's *not* a ring—not yet—so don't freak out, but I wanted to get you something pretty," and I open the small box he hands me, and it's a pink-enameled stiletto sandal on a gold chain.

"Because that's about fifty percent of what you were wearing the second time I ever saw you," he says.

"Pres."

"You're crying again. Did I screw up?"

"No. It's fucking perfect. The only thing that would have been more perfect would have been a small gold axe. Or a Nerf blaster."

"I thought about it. I really did. Also," he murmurs, "I feel like it's important to say that the only reason I'm not kissing you right now is that I'm ninety-five percent sure that I wouldn't be able to make it family friendly."

"Oh, I *definitely* wouldn't," I say.

We smolder at each other until Sonya says, "Enough of that! Come break the piñata!" So I do.

50

PRESTON

"**O**ut," Hanna says.

"There's still a lot of cleanup," I tell her.

"Leave. Begone."

"Are you quoting *Professor Wormbog in Search for the Zipperump-a-Zoo?*"

"No. I'm telling you that you need to take Natalie and go do whatever it is that my brothers do with the women they love when they're well out of range of both my sight and my hearing, and I don't want to know anything at all about it."

Natalie makes a small sound that I can't identify.

"You should go," Sonya says more kindly and gently. "We have this."

"I made the mess," I protest.

"You made the grand gesture," Shane says. "Go have makeup sex."

The sound Natalie makes this time is distinctly a choking sound. I'm hoping it's laughter and not disgust with my family. Because if I have my way, she's stuck with them.

We say goodbye and go out.

"I'm so sorry about them," I say when we reach the parking lot.

"They're perfect," she says. "I love them. Also, are they wrong?" She gives me a saucy look.

"No," I say. "They're right. But I have a few things I want to say before—"

"Before what?" she teases.

I lean in, whispering against her ear. "Before I make you scream my name while I'm buried to the hilt inside you."

I pull back to see her eyes go dark and her cheeks pink up. It's the prettiest thing I've ever seen.

"Better start talking," she says.

We're walking along the path back to the lodge, but I stop her and face her. "I was so busy trying to prove to my grandfather that I was good at what I do that I never took a second to ask myself if I liked what I do. When I went back, I realized that the way I live in New York, it's like—it's like Dorothy in Kansas. Black and white. And being here, with you, it's like Oz. All color. Vivid. Real. I had to go back to New York City to see the difference, and when I did—I can't stay there. Not without you."

"But I could come there," she says. "I would come there. To be with you. If that's what you wanted. I'm sure I could find the kind of work I like to do, and I'd make New York work for me."

"I know you would," I tell her. "You'd find a way to be happy anywhere, and you'd have enough left over to make the people around you happy, too. But that's not what I want for either of us. I want this. I want us to be surrounded by people who love us, in a place that both of us love."

"I want that, too," she says. "But what will you do here?"

"Truth?" I ask.

"Truth," she says.

"I don't have to do anything if I don't want to."

She opens her mouth. Then closes it again. "That must be nice."

"You don't have to, either."

She grins at that. "Are you offering to keep me?"

"I guess I kind of am."

"Do I seem like the kept type to you?"

I shake my head. "Not in the slightest. And I don't think I am, either. I think I need to be busy. But I don't know with what yet. Maybe it's helping to run the family business—if Hanna will even let me—maybe it's ranching, maybe it's finance. Maybe it's none of those things. But I want to give it the space to be its own thing. And—I want to do it with you by my side. That's the one thing I know."

She smiles at me and takes my hands. I love the feel of her fingers wrapped around mine. It's safety and excitement and fun all at the same time, and I don't remember the last time I felt that way. I know I was a kid. It was a long time ago. And it's so fucking good to feel it again.

She tilts her head against my arm, a trusting lean. "While you were gone, I realized that I needed to stop wanting to fix my life to match my mother's vision. I realized that *my* vision is the only one that matters. I was—going to come tell you that. And to tell you that you *were* the biggest and best part of what I envisioned for myself."

"Natalie—"

She pulls me down, and I kiss her. Hard.

"I told her that, too. We talked, and…I walked away at the end of the conversation. I don't know if that's it for us, or what. But I think I'm okay either way."

I give her a big hug. She feels amazing in my arms, curvy and alive and strong, her body relaxing and softening into our embrace. I can feel my own muscles tighten in answer, and her thigh presses a little closer.

"You really quit your job?" she asks. "Before you even knew if I wanted us to be together?"

I nod. "I did it for me. Because I don't need a decision I made years ago in anger to be the last word on what I want from my life."

"If you end up wanting to go back to New York—"

"*If* that happens, we'll talk about it," I tell her. "We'll make a decision together. But it won't be to prove something. It'll be because it's what I want and what works for *us*."

"Us," she repeats with wonder in her voice.

I cup her head gently and stand there a moment. I want my mouth on hers so much it feels like hunger, but the anticipation is so good, I don't want that to end, either.

She's the one who pulls me down, making a little greedy sound as our lips meet. Hers part, and I groan into her mouth.

"We should—"

She makes a gesture toward the lodge, tilting her head to one side. "I'd say your place or mine, but I'm guessing—"

"'Mine' right now is the guest room at Hanna's."

"And given that your plans for me involved me

screaming your name while you were—what?—'buried in me to the hilt'?"

The words in her desire-roughened voice wrap themselves around my cock, and another groan husks out of me.

"C'mon," she says and takes my hand.

51

NATALIE

If you'd asked me to picture makeup sex, I guess I would have said slow and tender. Or maybe really intense—some angst, a bunch of eye contact.

But Preston?

Wants to play.

And I am so, so here for it.

As soon as the door closes behind us, Preston kisses me. The briefest, lightest touch. Then again, teasing. Nipping. Pulling away as soon as I try to get more. He grins at me, and I can't help smiling back, overcome, as I so frequently am with him, by how much I like him.

He kisses me again, harder, but as soon as I try to deepen the kiss, he draws away. Kisses a line from the sensitive shell of my ear along my tingling jawline to my mouth —but won't kiss my mouth.

I groan and reach for him, but he angles my hands out of the way, not letting me touch him, not letting me grab at his clothes.

"Oh, so that's how it is?" I tease.

"I missed you," he says simply. "I missed playing with you. I missed how fun you are."

"Not just fun, though, right?" I ask, doubt crowding in.

He draws back so he can read my face—and that's what it is. A long, slow perusal, like he's trying to understand exactly what I need.

"Is that what you're afraid of?" he asks.

I nod.

"That this is just a *good times* thing?"

I nod again.

"Because that asshole…?"

I nod until my neck hurts.

"I'm not him," he says. "This is a *good times* thing and a *bad times* thing. It's a fun thing and a serious thing." He's quiet for a second, letting me see how much he means it, holding my gaze with his. "It's *everything*. I love all the things you are, Natalie."

Then he kisses me again, long and hard and sweet, a kiss I feel all the way to my core and in every nerve ending. When we break it to breathe, I say, "It's everything for me, too." And then, "But we can play if you want to play."

That makes him laugh. "I do," he says, and then he backs me toward the bed and tips me over onto it, crawling over me.

"You're wearing way too many clothes," he says and starts trying to wrestle me out of them. I fight back, going after his clothes, too, and we're laughing and wrestling and tangling ourselves up. At some point, breathless, we find ourselves naked, and he lowers himself over me, kissing me, his hard, muscular body smooth and hot except where his hair tickles and abrades me exactly right.

And now neither of us is laughing, though we're still breathless.

He's serious for a split second, eyes on mine: "You want this?"

"I want this," I say.

"Say 'pastry' if you need an out," he says, reaching for a condom and rolling it on, gaze dark and fierce in a way that makes my whole body hot.

"Got it," I say, and then he's on me, growling, pinning me, while I struggle under him. And it feels so good, the play, the resistance, his weight. So good, too good, his cock hard as fuck and grinding down on me, right where I need him, his chest hair rubbing my nipples, and I'm already coming for him.

He tests me with two fingers, licks them clean with his eyes sharp on my face, watching my reaction—and you'd think I'd be too satisfied and boneless, but I feel that lick and suck all the way down, a hot clench of my inner muscles, and I moan and part my legs for him.

"Yeah?" he says.

"Yeah," I tell him.

But it's not enough for him.

"I want to hear you say it," he says.

"I want you inside me," I say.

"Say it dirtier," he instructs.

I grin at him. "Or?"

"Or I won't do it."

"Preston Hott," I say, "you are the most fun *ever*." And I whisper into his ear, "I need you to fuck me right now, you hear me?"

And because this man is fun just for me, he does.

EPILOGUE

NATALIE—A BUNCH OF WEEKS LATER

Preston slings a zinger across the surface of the air hockey table. It slides into my goal, and he gives a quiet yelp of triumph.

I sigh.

Here's the thing.

It didn't take Preston long to become a superstar at fun.

He needed an outlet for his competitive spirit, since he's not helping companies devour other companies and gunning for a promotion—and apparently his outlet is...

Everything.

Which, don't get me wrong, I *love* it. I love anyone who takes a game seriously. I love a real competitor. I love the way his competitive spirit riles mine.

I just hate losing.

And the look he gives me right now tells me he knows it.

"Quit it," I grumble, but we both know I don't mean it. We also both know I'll reap my reward later when he'll make sure we both "win" in bed. And have plenty of fun.

Preston and I always have amazing sex, but we have the best sex after we've been sparring all night, like we have at the arcade, jockeying for first place.

At first when Preston moved back to Rush Creek, I stayed at the lodge, and he rented a sweet condo downtown. But then he started talking about the possibility of us moving in together. I resisted because it was hard for me to imagine how we'd find a place that fit both our budgets. After a few days of back and forth, he came up with a plan I adore: We'll split costs based on our respective net worths. It's only fair, after all. And, you know, he loves keeping the spreadsheets, and I love watching his forearms while he does it.

So we're buying this incredible house with a gorgeous view of the mountains. It's a pretty small house for a gadjillionaire and a pretty big house for a broke activities planner...but we both love it and can't wait to move in.

I stayed away from my mom for a little while, but a couple of weeks after she confronted me in the parking lot, she showed up to a Learn to Crochet class, which, if you know my mom, is one of the more improbable things that could happen. She sat quietly crocheting all night, and at the end, she came up to me and said, "I don't want to lose you."

I stared at her. Then she said, "I didn't think I wanted to crochet, but it was...kind of...fun."

She said the word *fun* like it was slightly dirty, so I stared at her for a while longer.

Eventually, she bit her lip, and looking more uncertain than I'd *ever* seen her, she said, "I was wrong, and I'm sorry. And I do. Want you to be happy, I mean."

I accepted her apology, warily, and we're working our way back to each other. Slowly. She's told me a little about how she grew up—in a house where her father controlled everything and her mother bowed to his iron will—and how she vowed to have enough power and money never to let that happen to her.

I still haven't told her what I overheard as a teenager, but the therapist I started seeing about my mom issues thinks it's not a bad idea, so maybe I will someday. I'm not quite ready to care what my mother thinks of me—and I might never be again—but...well, she cooks a mean roast, and I'm totally not the type to cut off my hand to spite my face.

Meanwhile, Preston has been taking things slowly, too, trying to figure out what he wants to do next. I know not to rush him. He's got plenty of money, and right now he's glorying in actually having *time*, which—he tells me—he wants to spend with the woman he loves. Sometimes he wanders the land pondering various things he could do with it. One day it's dude ranching, another it's small-scale farming, another it's expanding Hott Springs Eternal and building more event spaces.

He'll figure it out.

He hired Franklin away from Grantham-Hoyer and brought him out to Rush Creek, where he'll continue to be Preston's assistant on whatever project Preston undertakes next. And also, in case we need Italian pastries.

In other Hott news—and I mean that in every sense of the word—Rhys got his letter, the dreaded one from his granddad's will. It was quite a scene, which none of us actually witnessed, because...

Well, let's just say that our resident cynic landed waist deep in his least favorite thing: weddings. And that the wedding he was tasked with planning belongs to one of his least favorite people, the sunny, eternally optimistic divorcee whose ex-husband he represented in their divorce a couple of years back.

The rest of us are munching popcorn and trying to figure out how he's going to survive Fox Hott's latest round of shenanigans.

Preston holds up his arcade swipe card. "How about we have a rematch—winner gets to be on top," he says.

That makes me laugh.

"How about we have a rematch—winner has to be on the bottom?" I counter.

He stalks around the table, bends down, and sets his mouth right by my ear. "How about winner fucks the loser very slowly and very deeply from behind while she's braced over a big stack of pillows?"

"There are a lot of assumptions built into that," I say breathlessly.

"Well," he says. "All good analysis starts with some assumptions."

My body has lost all definition, drawn gravitationally to his.

"Family place," he reminds me, before dropping a chaste kiss onto my cheek.

"Game on," I tell him.

He beats me soundly, but I can't find it in me to care.

ACKNOWLEDGMENTS

Thank you to everyone who has read, and loved, and told me how much you love the Wilders and the Hotts. I do this for you, and you make it a delight to do.

A huge thank you to my early readers, Brenda St. John Brown, Christina Hovland, Rachel Grant, Liz Alden, Christine D'Abo, and Kate Davies. It's so much easier to write a book with you as my friends and allies. I don't know what I'd do without you.

So many thanks also to the author friends who support me on a regular basis—those I've already mentioned, as well as the authors in RAM Rom Com, ECRW, my various Discord servers, and many, many more, including but not limited to Jen Pitts, Chrissy Elliot, the rest of the the Starbucks crew, the writers of BARN, Julie Farley, Kris Kennedy, Gwen Hernandez, Audrey Nelson, Jessica Auerbach, Cheryl Cain, the Good Eggs, and my romance and indie roundtable peeps.

Thank you to my agent, Emily Sylvan Kim, and my sub rights agent, Tina Shen.

Thank you, Mandi Andrejka of Inky Pen Editing. You hold all of Rush Creek (and a healthy helping of my sanity) in your brain, your style sheets, and your lovely Aeon file, and I don't take any of it for granted.

Thank you, Chloe Alvarez, for capturing Preston and Natalie in your fantastic illustration, and for the fun collaboration!

Thank you, XPresso Book Tours, especially Giselle, for the release blitz.

Hugs and kisses for my not-author friends who support my imaginary worlds with so much love and patience: Aimee, Darya, Ellen, Elizabeth, Lauren, Molly, Soomie, and Tracey.

To BellGirl, BellBoy, and Mr. Bell, thank you for being the best family in the world, better than any I could imagine, and also realer. I love you all so much.

Any errors of fact or insensitivity relating to representation are mine and mine alone. If you note any, please let me know so I can fix them and learn to do better.

ALSO BY SERENA BELL

Wilder Adventures

Make Me Wilder

Walk on the Wilder Side

Wilder With You

A Little Wilder

Wilder at Last

Hott Springs Eternal

Hott Shot

Hott Take

Some Like It Hott

Running Hott

Under One Roof

Do Over

Head Over Heels

Sleepover

Returning Home

Hold On Tight

Can't Hold Back

To Have and to Hold

Holding Out

Tierney Bay

So Close

So True

New York Glitz

Still So Hot!

Hot & Bothered

Standalone

Turn Up the Heat

ABOUT THE AUTHOR

USA Today bestselling author Serena Bell writes contemporary romance with heat, heart, and humor. A former journalist, Serena has always believed that everyone has an amazing story to tell if you listen carefully, and you can often find her scribbling in her tiny garret office, main-lining chocolate and bringing to life the tales in her head.

Serena's books have earned many honors, including a RITA finalist spot, an RT Reviewers' Choice Award, Apple Books Best Book of the Month, and Amazon Best Book of the Year for Romance.

When not writing, Serena loves to spend time with her college-sweetheart husband and two hilarious kiddos—all of whom are incredibly tolerant not just of Serena's imaginary friends but also of how often she changes her hobbies and how passionately she embraces the new ones. These days, it's quilting, pickle ball, board-gaming, meditation, and long walks with good friends.